KV-307-407

Woodturning
Music Boxes

Woodturning Music Boxes

James A. Jacobson

Sterling Publishing Co., Inc. New York
Distributed in the U.K. by Blandford Press

ACKNOWLEDGMENTS

The author wishes to thank and acknowledge the Swiss music movement manufacturer Reuge for permission to photograph its movements and for information provided to assist in manuscript development.

The invaluable photographic work of Peter J. Jacobson is recognized with great appreciation.

Library of Congress Cataloging in Publication Data

Jacobson, James A.
  Woodturning music boxes.

  Includes index.
  1. Music box. 2. Music box—Construction.
I. Title.
ML1066.J3 1983   789'.8   83-4673
ISBN 0-8069-7726-4 (pbk.)

Copyright © 1983 by Sterling Publishing Co., Inc.
Two Park Avenue, New York, N.Y. 10016
Distributed in Australia by Oak Tree Press Co., Ltd.
P.O. Box K514 Haymarket, Sydney 2000, N.S.W.
Distributed in the United Kingdom by Blandford Press
Link House, West Street, Poole, Dorset BH15 1LL, England
Distributed in Canada by Oak Tree Press Ltd.
℅ Canadian Manda Group, P.O. Box 920, Station U
Toronto, Ontario, Canada M8Z 5P9
Manufactured in the United States of America
All rights reserved

CONTENTS

Dedicated
to
Anita, Karen, Peter, Ann and Chris
and, of course, Christin Ann

Woodturning
Music Boxes

FOREWORD

In his book *Positive Addiction**, Dr. William Glasser articulates the need for people to become addicted to behaviors that are growth-producing, that make life more satisfying and meaningful. While Glasser does not refer to it, nothing can encourage and sustain a positive addiction like the wood lathe. The turning of wood is a behavior unequalled by any other method of working wood.

While leaning a bit towards an overstatement, the above does make my biases conspicuous regarding the lathe. For the hobbyist, it can be the mechanism for constructively using leisure time. For the professional turner, the wood lathe is the vehicle for immense personal satisfaction and growth.

As delightful as it is, one of the dilemmas of the turner's craft is the persistent question: What is it for? While the nonfunctional wood object can obviously stand by itself without embarrassment, the woodturner's detractors raise a valid question. While enlightenment may be the long-term answer, some alternative approaches with the turned object may also address the question.

Having turned innumerable hardwood boxes or containers with lids, seemingly with no obvious function, I began to sense a legitimacy to the question of purpose. The result of my own conceptual but very pragmatic meanderings was the linking of high-quality clockwork music movements and the turned hardwood box. Two very important addictions in my own life seemed to blend to answer, at least in part, the question of purpose for me. The pleasure of wood and music is an incredible combination! I hope, through this volume on how to make your own lathed music boxes, you will experience some of this pleasure too.

---

*Glasser, William, *Positive Addiction*. New York: Harper & Row, 1976.

INTRODUCTION

The linking of wood to clockwork music movements via the lathe presents the woodturner with an adventure in fascination and satisfaction. It's an undertaking that is accessible to the beginning turner and challenging to the experienced. Turning music boxes with lids confronts the turner not only with the demands of the wood but the task of integrating the music movement into a functioning wood piece.

My initial attempts at turning round music boxes emerged from the production turning of lathed hardwood containers with lids. While the boxes were well turned from superb woods, another dimension seemed necessary for completeness. Essentially, I was seeking something that would make the boxes functional but yet would not distract from the wood. A long-standing interest in music and, in particular, clockwork music, provided the solution to the problem.

Generally, music boxes have been designed employing squares or rectangles. Since music movements are crafted or manufactured for placement in nonround objects, a number of problems presented themselves. The lathed box required a diameter of sufficient size to accommodate the movement, initially an 18-note movement. While standardization does exist among movement manufacturers, it does not exist between them. The issue of diameter and other dimensions and measurement problems was finally solved by selecting movements produced by only one manufacturer.

Another major problem that needed to be addressed was the sounding board that music movements require. As mass-produced music boxes are manufactured from basswood, including the sounding board, a crude sound test was employed. Since basswood is a soft hardwood, it was assumed that the harder the wood used the more effective would be the sounding board. This assumption proved accurate, based on a number of experiments and subsequent experience with boxes from various hardwoods.

Closely related to questions about the sounding board was the problem of the extended winding mechanism that most music movements require. While winding keys of various lengths can be obtained, the winding shaft itself generally protrudes approximately one-quarter inch from the base of the movement. As you will discover, a hole must be drilled through the sounding board for insertion of the winding shaft. However, the base of the box must be open to allow for winding and free movement of the winding key. This problem was eventually solved by using a standardized key length and making a lathe chuck for tooling out the base of the box.

What seemed like an insolvable problem was how to design the box so that the music movement would turn on or off with the lid. After many attempts ended in utter failure, the task was approached differently. Rather than attempt to replicate an on/off mechanism that was designed for square or rectangle boxes, an entirely different mechanism was required for a round music box. Also, to maintain the integrity of the wood, it was determined that the usual metal springs and wires should not be employed in the lathed box. Additional experience in making the music boxes has led to the development and identification of a number of very functional on/off mechanisms for round pieces. These will be detailed in the step-by-step directions provided in later chapters.

While other problems remained to be solved, once those primary ones were addressed the excitement of turning music boxes with lids began. As you will discover, thanks to the lathe, the design possibilities are endless. Also, the total array of hardwoods lends itself to lathed music boxes. As you begin to identify the sources of music movements, you will be amazed at the multitude of tunes and movements that are available in clockwork music. Recently, I have attempted to design and lathe boxes in relation to the type of music played by the movement. More about this later.

As music movements represent an area where most turners lack familiarity, I provide the reader with detailed information. As indicated earlier, the turner will very quickly come to appreciate the superb craftsmanship contained in high-quality music movements. Considerable material, including photographs and diagrams, is presented to assist in understanding all that is necessary to integrate music movements into lathed boxes.

Chapter 1, dealing with clockwork music movements, will also focus on the other primary resource required: the woods. While it is assumed that the reader has some knowledge of both hardwoods and softwoods, some information will be provided based on my own experience. Chapters 1 and 2 contain extensive bibliographies for your additional reading. While literature related to music movements is rather limited, some that should prove helpful have been identified and listed. References related to wood are, in general, those publications that I have found helpful and informative over the years.

Woodturning will be discussed along with appropriate tools and chucks that will be helpful in making music boxes and bowls. Since there are numerous excellent books on turning techniques and methods, I will spend a minimum of time on these concerns. I will, however, share a few of my own methods specific to faceplate-turning boxes and bowls. Also, the necessary chucks and other handy devices I use will be pictured and detailed. That chapter is accompanied by a rather thorough bibliography of what I have found to be outstanding books on woodturning and related concerns.

Each of the subsequent chapters details, with photographs and directions, step-by-step procedures for faceplate-turning both musical boxes and lids, musical bowls, placement of the music movement, and other information that will assist you in your tasks. The chapters are laid out to progress from a rather elementary design requiring limited turning skills to the more complex. None of the box or bowl designs presented is beyond the reach of the hobbyist woodturner. While it may at times seem redundant, I persist in reminding the turner of safety issues in woodturning.

Music Movements
and Wood

Chapter 1

MUSIC MOVEMENTS AND WOOD

There is a certain magnetic fascination about some things that we encounter in our world, especially when we take the time to have another look. We discover that the more intensively we examine and experience these things, the more fascinated we become with them. Wood is unquestionably one of the things that captivates and pulls us back for another look.

Music is another. For those who have encountered the sounds of clockwork music, the magnetism is irresistible. Those who look again are captivated even further by the craftsmanship and intricacies of music movements.

To link together that which is so uniquely natural and that which is truly human, affords the woodturner a fascinating task. For those who are addicted to the lathe or those who are approaching it for the first time, the integration of a superbly crafted musical instrument into a wood container, shaped at will, is a task worthy of pursuit. But to transform fascination to understanding, some information is necessary.

The History of Music Movements

From Anton Favre to the Present

The origin of cylinder music movements, their development and eventual production is closely intertwined with horology, i.e., the art of clockmaking. While the basic principles of mechanically produced sound can be traced back to the ancients, these principles were maximized by 18th and 19th century European craftsmen. Most historians of both horology and cylinder musical movements seem to credit Geneva, Switzerland, as the cradle of the music box. While our primary concern is with cylinder musical movements, we will make reference to disc musical movements and also to Thomas Edison's inventions. Edison's inventions and the development of the recorder or graphophone brought an end to the production of the large, extraordinarily high-quality cylinder musical movements.

Before proceeding further in detailing and exploring the history of cylinder movements, you should have some working knowledge of the various musical movement components, their names and function. The invention of the musical box seems more the product of many craftsmen developing and refining the various components than of one person making a singular discovery. Familiarity with the various component parts is critical to understanding the historical development of the musical movement. Also, knowledge of the various parts and their function will serve you well as you begin working with movements to place in your lathed containers.

One brief language lesson is in order before examining the movement and its primary parts. Arthur W. J. G. Ord-Hume, one of the foremost authorities on the history of musical boxes, points out that the word "music" is a noun and its adjective form is "musical." Thus, when a box plays music it becomes, properly, a musical box rather than a music box. Common usage, especially in the United States, suggests that both references are acceptable. Frequently I will use the terms interchangeably, as do other writers, as well as both the manufacturers and distributors of musical movements.

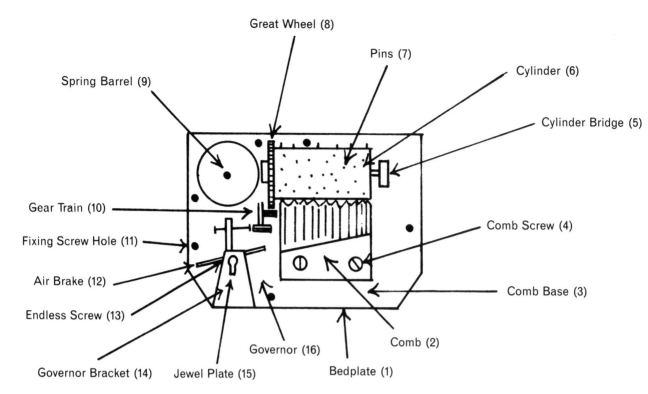

Illus. 1-1 Diagram of Music Movement Components

Illus. 1-1 presents the basic components of a keywound cylinder music movement in its simplest form. Each component is subsequently described in terms of function.

(1) Bedplate. The bedplate is the metal base of the movement to which all the other components are attached. In early movements the bedplates were generally made from brass, cast iron, and, in some instances, steel. Later bedplates were made from zinc and zinc alloys. Current bedplates on movements are from an alloy. The size and thickness of the bedplate are important as it is the bedplate that transmits the tonal vibrations created by the movement to the box or bowl that houses the unit. This is critical both in terms of volume and quality of sound.

(2) Comb. The comb is made of metal teeth (spring steel) that are the primary means of producing the musical sounds of the movement. The individual teeth of the comb are tuned to a musical scale ranging from bass to treble. The musical sound is produced when the teeth are struck and slightly lifted by pins on the cylinder, dropped and set in vibration. Most combs have what are called dampers on the teeth, especially on the bass teeth, to limit the extent of their vibration. If they vibrated too long, they would distort the musical sound. Musical movements are generally described by the number of teeth in the comb.

(3) Comb Base. The comb base is a portion of the bedplate but is elevated to hold the comb securely and in alignment with the cylinder and its pins.

(4) Comb Screws. These are the screws that hold the comb securely to the comb base. Since the comb must be aligned with the pins on the cylinder, the comb screws allow for the loosening and necessary movement of the comb for this process. After alignment has been achieved, the screws are tightened to prevent movement of the comb.

(5) Cylinder Bridge. Literally a metal bridge,

the cylinder bridge is a portion of the bedplate that supports one end of the cylinder. The bridge contains a metal shaft that supports but yet allows free movement of the cylinder.

(6) Cylinder. Through a series of precisely placed steel pins on or in its surface, the cylinder determines the musical tune that the movement will play. A different cylinder, at least in small movements, is required for each tune because the pins must be placed in different positions. Early (and also current) movements were crafted with one fixed cylinder. Later developments led to interchangeable cylinders that allowed for playing more than one tune on the same basic movement. Generally the cylinders are made from or finished with brass.

(7) Pins. Small, steel pins on the cylinder surface lift and activate the vibrations of the teeth of the comb. The pins are placed in different positions on the cylinder depending on the tune that is to be played.

(8) Great Wheel. Generally the great wheel is that large geared wheel at the end of the cylinder that is activated by the ratchets of the winding or spring mechanism. The great wheel is the first in the movement's gear train.

(9) Spring Barrel. The spring barrel houses the spring that is wound, generally by a key, that makes the movement of the mechanism possible.

(10) Gear Train. The gear train is the balance of the geared wheels and pinions that run off the great wheel. They are necessary for controlling and, with the governor, maintaining the movement at the proper speed.

(11) Fixing Screw Hold. This hole is threaded to receive the fixing screw that holds the movement to the base of the box or bowl. Most movements have three or more fixing holes, depending upon the size of the movement.

(12) Air Brake. The primary function of the air brake is to assist in controlling the speed of the movement. It is also called the "butterfly" and the "flywheel." Fine adjustments, especially on the larger movements, in the speed of the movement can be made by adjusting the wings. Most on/off

mechanisms used with movements rely on the air brake to function. To stop the movement from playing, a shaft or wire intercepts and stops the air brake from moving and thereby shuts down the movement. To permit the movement to continue playing, the air brake is released.

(13) Endless Screw. The endless screw is a worm gear that holds and drives the air brake. This screw is a critical component of the overall governor of the movement that controls and maintains its speed.

(14) Governor Bracket. This bracket holds the endless screw and the air brake in place. It contains a small hole that is a receptacle for the tip of the endless screw. The bracket is also called the "cock."

(15) Jewel Plate. The jewel plate is a strip of metal attached to the top of the governor bracket to hold the endless screw in place. In early movements it literally held a jewel on which the endless screw would freely and quietly revolve.

(16) Governor. The governor is that part of the movement that is responsible for controlling the speed of the movement. In most movements it consists of the governor bracket, the endless screw, the air brake, a geared wheel that turns the endless screw, and a shaft and pinion that connects to the gear train.

In that the history and development of the musical box is well documented by a number of historians, our exploration will focus more on those specific details and aspects of the history that seem especially interesting. I have provided a rather extensive bibliography where the reader can pursue, in greater depth, what one writer has called "the curious history of the musical box" [Mosoriak, 1943].

There seems little disagreement among historians that the cylinder musical movement developed rather gradually in the western part of Switzerland. One of the more renowned historians, L. G. Jaccard, who was also a crafter and repairer of musical movements, suggests that the development of the musical movement began about 1750. He indicates that its early development took place in the area of western Switzerland bordering France that is called the Valley of Joux (La Vallée de Joux). This area, both in the mid-18th century and for many years following, was noted for its expert watchmakers. As the watchmakers worked independently in what was apparently a highly competitive business, they were very secretive about any new technologies they developed. Thus, Jaccard suggests, while the beginnings of the musical movement definitely came from these watchmakers, it is impossible to identify any one horologist as the primary inventor [Jaccard, IMBS].

Some historians, along with current tourist literature provided by various governmental agencies, attribute the invention of the musical movement to Anton Favre. Favre, a Swiss watchmaker in Geneva, is credited with having invented the flexible steel tooth comb in 1796. More specifically, Arthur W.J.G. Ord-Hume suggests that Favre was "the progenitor of the stacked comb." The stacked comb, in music movements, had the teeth placed one on top of the other to allow for placement in watches. Favre integrated his newly designed comb into one of his watches. There also is some evidence to suggest that Favre miniaturized the comb and other music movement components to fit into a watch. While the resolution of this historical issue of who invented the musical movement remains uncertain, it is clear that the development of the comb with flexible steel teeth was the prime factor in the emergence of the musical movement industry.

As the technology of the musical movement developed, the watchmakers from western Switzerland began to migrate to Geneva in the early years of the 19th century. Because of its size, its resources, and its accessibility to larger commercial markets, Geneva became the early center of musical movement manufacturing. Thus, most historians consider Geneva, as indicated earlier, the cradle of the music box industry.

While Geneva continued as a focal point of musical box manufacturing, the city of Ste.-Croix in the Jura Mountains began to develop its own musical movement industry. Jaccard credits Abram Louis Cuendet with the primary responsibility for initiating the industry in Ste.-Croix. Historically, Ste.-Croix had been involved in crafting superb watches and clocks, thus it possessed the skilled craftsmen who could easily move to the manufacture of musical movements. It is interesting to note that Ste.-Croix is currently the primary manufacturing center of high-quality musical movements.

Until approximately 1820 the combs used in music movements were made up of individual teeth. Each tooth was separately crafted, and attached to the baseplate of the unit. A significant development, attributed to David Lecoultre of Geneva, was the process of manufacturing the combs from a single piece of steel. This discovery apparently enabled the manufacturers to reduce substantially the amount of handwork, and corresponding expense, that was involved in the older single-tooth method. Historians also credit Lecoultre with the development of the cylinder and the placement of it parallel to the comb.

While much of the work involved in musical box production was a "cottage industry," engaged in by many residents of both Geneva and Ste.-Croix, many parts were manufactured by factories not directly involved in the industry. The basic components were manufactured, but the skilled craftsmen and the cottage industry were needed to transform them into the finished parts for the movements. Until 1875, when the first production-line musical-movement factory was established, most movements were primarily crafted and assembled by hand. While numerous specialized tools were developed and available, their use required highly skilled craftsmen. It's interesting to note the various job titles and functions of those early workers, both men and women; Alfred Chapuis details some of them in his informative book *History of the Musical Box and of Mechanical Music*.

The early foundries in both Ste.-Croix and Geneva produced the bedplates, cylinders, and governors. According to Chapuis these manufacturers were referred to as "blank-makers." Others engaged in specific tasks had titles appropriate to their functions as well. The person responsible for identifying where the steel pins were to be placed on the cylinder was called "the pricker." Using a highly specialized tool called a "piquage" (Chapuis reports), the pricker would mark the exact position on the cylinder where each pin was to be placed. The pricker would work from the musical score of the tune that the cylinder was to play when the movement was complete. The work was painstaking at best and required extraordinary skill and concentration.

Another highly skilled job that Chapuis identifies was done by a craftsman called the "pinner." The cylinder, after it was properly marked by the pricker, would be passed to the pinner, whose primary function was to drill holes in the cylinder at those exact points marked by the pricker. It was also the responsibility of the pinner, using a tweezer, to place the steel cylinder pins in the holes, a highly tedious task. It is worth noting at this point that the early movements that would play one musical tune could have anywhere from 800 to 1000 separate pins in the cylinder. The larger cylinders that played multiple tunes required many thousands of pins. Such a number of pins gives an indication of the nature of the pinner's task.

The next major craftsman involved in the process Chapuis identifies as "the poseur, the comb-setter." His essential function seems to have been to straighten the teeth of the comb and to be certain they were in perfect alignment with the pins of the cylinder. A job closely related to the comb-setter was that of "the tuner," who would use a "master comb" that was perfectly tuned. With a file, the tuner would remove metal from each tooth until it sounded exactly like its counterpart in the master comb.

Prior to final assembly and the finishing process, a craftsman using what was called a "bender" had to put a slight bend in each of the steel pins on the cylinder. It was necessary to bend all pins slightly so that they would properly lift the teeth of the comb as the cylinder rotated. The magnitude of this task can be realized by recalling the number of steel pins on each cylinder. Chapuis also says that this person had to verify that the pins were correctly placed on the cylinder; in a sense he was responsible for inspection and quality control of the work done by those craftsmen who preceded him.

Two important jobs remained in the process. Chapuis discusses "the assembler," who had the task of taking the entire mechanism apart, checking and aligning each component, and reassembling the unit. When he was through, the reassembled movement was given to "the finisher."

First task of the finisher was to place dampers on certain teeth of the comb. The dampers, as suggested earlier, would control the extent of vibration of the tooth after it was struck by a cylinder pin. Dampers were especially critical on the longer, thicker bass teeth, and were, essentially, small steel springs. The treble teeth on the comb, at least the larger ones, would have dampers made from feathers or parchment paper. The dampers were (and still are) placed on the underside of the teeth near their tips. The final task of the finisher was to align the comb and its teeth with the cylinder and its pins. Each tooth had to be in perfect alignment with the pins that were to pluck it. Also, the pins would have to lift the teeth of the comb to a specific height or the tone produced would be very harsh in sound. Thus, the teeth could only overlap the pins by a very specific distance.

Another interesting aspect of the history of musical movements was that early in their development small musical movements were placed in watches, cane handles, bottles, and jewelry boxes. Jaccard relates that movements were also commonly placed in snuff boxes, more appropriately called "tabatières." The snuff boxes were so popular that, according to Jaccard, this type of small cylinder musical box, no matter what its use, became known as the tabatière. This term for the small cylinder music boxes was retained down through the history of the musical movement.

While popular, Mosoriak, in *The Curious History of Music Boxes*, suggests that these small music movements were "pip-squeaks" that produced only a very small volume of sound with not a great deal of quality. Obviously the buying public of the time disagreed with Mosoriak's assessment.

During this early period of the 19th century, the Swiss craftsmen also developed what was called the "manivelle." The manivelle was a crank-type movement that was easy to produce and low in cost. The early manivelles, as they are today, were primarily used in children's toys. The mechanism was a worm screw, a large gear wheel, the cylinder and comb. Unlike current crank-type movements, many of the early manivelles could play multiple tunes.

It's worth noting that the early small movements (the tabatières) and the manivelles were not prohibitively expensive for the average person. Frequently, however, when they were expensive it was the result of the quality of and elaborate decorations on the box or object that the movement was placed in.

Ord-Hume notes that the first wooden musical boxes appeared after about 1810. Apparently the boxes were quite plain and usually made from one of the area hardwoods. While Ord-Hume doesn't indicate the type of hardwood that was used, he does suggest that it was often so thick that it "tended to deaden the sound" of the movement. Reference is made to pine as being used effectively as base material or for sounding boards. The early boxes that also were designed with a lid and hinge system were usually finished with wax. Ord-Hume indicates the use of French polish in finishing music boxes came some years after the initial use of wood.

Graham Webb, in his book *The Cylinder Musical Box Handbook*, also discusses the early and later music boxes made from wood. He suggests that the early craftsmen were more concerned with the sound produced by the musical movement than with the box that housed it. The early wooden boxes would, however, often be made from hardwoods with attractive grains. Later, Webb indicates, when wood veneer and inlays became popular, the musical movement manufacturers brought cabinetmakers into their production systems, and sought to outdo one another with both the design and appearance of their wooden boxes. The historian reports that the most common veneer that the cabinetmakers used in the boxes was rosewood. He also points out that the box makers frequently avoided using mahogany and oak because they felt those two woods tended to deaden the musical sound. (I have not found this to be true.) It's also interesting to note that, although it was available as a production tool, no mention is made of wood-turning musical boxes with a lathe.

As interest and market demands increased for musical movements, the Geneva craftsmen developed and began manufacturing what was called the "cartel." Jaccard indicates that the cartel, or large-size cylinder musical box, was first introduced in 1833. With the introduction of the cartel, the music box industry moved into its most significant, profitable, and exciting period. It was a period that would last, according to Q. David Bowers in his *Encyclopedia of Automatic Musical Instruments*, until approximately 1895, during which time musical movements and boxes of such extraordinary quality, craftsmanship, and beauty were produced that they have become the treasures of museums and private collectors around the world.

It's worth noting at this point that while current musical movement manufacturers, especially the Swiss, produce a truly high-quality cylinder mechanism, there is little comparison between them and those crafted during the mid-19th century. In part, this can be explained by understanding the radical technological differences between that era and our own. Prior to 1877, when Edison invented the voice recorder and reproducer, music could only be heard and enjoyed while it was being played live. While there were many opportunities to hear live concerts and other music performances, there was no technology for the recording and subsequent reproduction of the music. Thus, the cylinder musical box with its portability, ease of operation, and capacity to perform at the will of the owner became highly desired. It allowed access to music whenever it was wanted. One of the cartels was called a "dinner box" because it was capable of playing continuously for a period of at least two hours. Such a box, at least for those who could afford it, literally provided the background music while the household dined.

The development of the cartel resulted in a series of new technologies being applied in the musical box industry. The cartel (the term is still used by European collectors), according to Jaccard, allowed for creating different tones and also more complex musical arrangements. One of the early cartels was called "the mandoline." According to Mosoriak, the mandoline box would repeat the dominant note a specific number of times and at fixed intervals, thus creating a sound similar to the stringed mandolin or lute. The true mandoline box, Ord-Hume reports, usually had approximately ninety teeth, and in some instances 180 teeth would be included in their combs. Other types of cartel boxes developed during this period was classified according to the type and arrangement of the music they played.

In addition to the mandoline there was also the "forte piano." It was called so because it was capable of playing music either loudly or softly. Another cartel was called the "flute" because it combined the use of reeds with the comb to create a sound similar to a flute. Actually the flute was an early version of another group of cartels called the "orchestra." The orchestra boxes integrated bells, wooden or metal whistles, drums, and, according to Jaccard, even, on occasion, castanets. These items combined with the comb and the cylinder of the movements create a sound similar to an orchestra.

As these very elaborate cartels developed, they became, as Ord-Hume reports, extremely expensive luxuries even for the affluent. Not only were the musical movements expensive but they were housed in very elaborate cases and, in some instances, exquisite cabinets and chests. Fortunately the manufactureres also continued to produce the smaller, less expensive boxes and movements.

Until about 1850, even though the cartels were superb mechanisms, enclosed in luxury, they could still only play the tunes that they were manufactured to play. While they could play a number of tunes from the same large cylinder, nonetheless the selection was always the same. Obviously the owners became tired of listening to them, despite the uniqueness of their sound. Then, about 1850, the "rechange" or changeable cylinder system was introduced by the makers of movements. Jaccard reports that this system provided a musical movement with, usually, six additional cylinders that could be played by the owner. The new capacity for more and different tunes was a significant advancement in both the industry and the marketplace, although a major drawback of the rechange system was that you had to buy the extra cylinders at the time you purchased the music movement. The cylinders were custom designed to fit only one specific movement.

The year 1878 saw the introduction of the "interchangeable cylinder" in the music movement industry. Unlike the rechange system, the manufacturers standardized their movements so that new cylinders could be ordered and used without having to purchase an entirely new unit. The owner could keep adding new cylinders to his musical holdings as long as he indicated to the manufacturer or supplier the appropriate number from his box.

Shortly after interchangeable cyliners were introduced, the largest of all musical boxes were produced. These large boxes were generally referred to as the "grand format." Arthur Ord-Hume reports that their movements had cylinders ranging from 18″ to 33″ in length with diameters from 4½″ to 6″. One manufacturer produced a grand format with cylinders 6′ long.

Most of the historians seem to agree that the period between 1880 and 1890 saw the decline of the cylinder musical box industry. Some suggest it was in part due to the poor quality of many of the movements that were being produced. Other historians suggest that the cylinder box had become so cheap and readily available that there remained little demand for them. Clearly the elaborate cartels could not maintain the industry, because only the very wealthy could afford them. More probably the demise of the cylinder industry was related to the new Edison inventions and also to the development of a new type of musical movement called the "disc" music box.

While our primary concern is with the cylinder musical box, a few observations about the disc movement seem appropriate. This type of music box played inexpensive, changeable flat tin discs. Their cost made possible what one writer called "music for the masses." The disc box employed a comb system that was activated by perforations in the disc. An English inventor named Ellis Parr and a Paul Lockman from Leipzig, Germany, are credited with the simultaneous invention of the disc system. As a result of this invention, the musical box industry shifted from Switzerland to Germany, to England, and eventually to the United States.

With the migration of German citizens to the United States who had expertise in disc music boxes, the industry was transplanted to this country. The famous Regina Company was established in New Jersey. Most historians and collectors seem to agree that the Regina was "the best disc musical box of all time."

While the cylinder music box industry was largely overshadowed by the disc boxes and other new sound-reproduction technologies, not all manufacturers went out of business (although some Swiss manufacturers went out of business as a result of World War I). Several have remained in operation and continue to produce high-quality cylinder musical movements. One current manufacturer is Thorens, established in the 1880s.

In addition to smaller cylinder movements, Thorens produces a five-cylinder, interchangeable-cylinder box that will play a total of twenty tunes. In recent years the company has reintroduced the production of the disc music box, and in addition to that movement Thorens also manufactures a substantial library of disc tunes that are available for its mechanism. Thorens also continues to produce the manivelle or crank-type music movement.

In recent years the Japanese have also entered the cylinder musical movement industry; their production has focused primarily on the smaller cylinder movements. The Sankyo, Fuji, and Seiki companies are three of a number of Japanese firms producing movements. It seems clear from the extent of production activity surrounding the musical box industry that the clockwork sound remains, for the present and foreseeable future, very popular and in demand.

One current manufacturer, Reuge S.A. of Switzerland, produces high-quality movements that I have used consistently in my lathed musical boxes and bowls. While I have used other movements, I have been especially satisfied with the Reuge cylinder movements. Thus, in presenting specific information about cylinder musical movements and how to use them in lathed boxes and bowls, I will use Reuge products as examples. Given this focus on Reuge movements, a brief glimpse at the history of the Reuge company is appropriate.

Charles Reuge, a maker of clocks and pocket watches, moved to the city of Ste.-Croix, Switzerland, in 1865. Apparently Reuge was attracted to Ste.-Croix because of its reputation for workmanship. Upon moving there, he decided to undertake the production of musical watches. Charles Reuge died prematurely, but in 1886 another member of the Reuge family, Albert, opened a factory in Ste.-Croix for the production of musical boxes. As the historians of Reuge indicate, the early years of the 20th century and of the First World War were extremely difficult ones not only for Reuge but for all other movement manufacturers. As you will recall, Edison's inventions had severe impact upon the former markets.

In the years that followed the First World War, Reuge and others began to prosper by developing more and different uses for their products. Following the death of Albert Reuge in 1929, his wife,

Alice, became the driving force behind the company. Under Alice Reuge the company constructed its first industrial buildings in 1930 and continued to expand and improve its production technology. Following the death of Alice Reuge in 1958, her three sons assumed responsibility for the company ["Brief History of Reuge S.A.," 1982].

Clockwork Music: The Unique Sound

The musical sound produced by steel pins plucking and setting in vibration tuned steel teeth has always fascinated me. I have found such great pleasure in this unique sound that it puzzles me that early manufacturers sought to produce movements that imitated other instruments. From my perspective, that which makes the musical box so enjoyable is the sound that it alone can create so well. What makes this sound even more satisfying is the visual pleasure you obtain when watching the mechanism perform.

Everyone in our society has heard the sound of clockwork music. Whether it emerges from the innards of a stuffed animal, from a gaudy ceramic cookie jar, or from a finely crafted walnut case, the sound is always recognized and it inevitably captures our attention. The clockwork sound seems to mandate a smile that the listener is compelled to give. It's interesting to note that the sound of the music movement has never been a respecter of age; both young and old somehow feel a bit happier or sadder, but certainly more alive as a result of an encounter with it. While it's difficult to explain the feelings generated by the sound, it's possible to describe how the clockwork sound is produced.

By definition, clockwork music is mechanically produced sound. Mosoriak suggests that it is music by means of vibrating tongues or teeth. As one begins to explore the principles and characteristics of sound, vibration is a recurring theme. By simple observation of the cylinder pins lifting the tuned teeth of the comb, one can sense that the sound is being produced by vibrations.

Alfred Chapuis presents a very informative discussion of sound as it relates to musical boxes in his *History of the Musical Box and of Mechanical Music*. To understand the clockwork sound, Chapuis suggests that you must be familiar with the tuning fork and how it works.

The basic principle of the tuning fork is that when it is struck it will vibrate with a specific number of vibrations per second and thus produce a specific tone. For example, Chapuis points out that "when the tuning fork sounds the note *la*, it does so at 870 simple vibrations per second." The number of vibrations produced by the tuning fork is determined, in part, by the length and thickness of the steel prongs. Large tuning forks vibrate more slowly, i.e. they vibrate fewer times per second and thus produce the lower or bass pitches. The smaller tuning forks vibrate more rapidly, i.e. they produce many vibrations per second and thus generate the higher or treble tones or pitches.

The teeth on the comb of the musical movement are basically small tuning forks, designed to vibrate a specific number of times when plucked by the pins, and thus produce a specific note. A major problem that confronted the early developers of the comb and teeth had to do with the bass sounds. To produce the bass sounds that the music required, the bass teeth would of necessity have been disproportionately long and thick. However, as Chapuis reports, "someone had the ingenious idea of substituting additional weight for length, thus slowing the speed of vibrations" and, as you might guess, producing the desired pitch.

When you look at the top of the comb teeth of a musical movement, you will note that they are all about the same length. However, you will also note the different width of the teeth between the treble and the bass. As you will recall, the thin teeth (less mass) produce the high tones (treble); the thick teeth (more mass) are the ones that produce the low tones (bass). Also, if you look under the teeth of the comb, you will note how the bass teeth are weighted with more metal than are the treble teeth.

A final thought. It's curious to observe that even

though I understand how the musical movement creates its music, the clockwork sound still shrouds itself with mystery and fascination. Clearly the clockwork sound, like all music, has to do with something far beyond the mechanics and principles of its production.

The Music Movement

Types of Movements and Music Available

There are any number of fine musical movements available today, but I will focus on the Reuge movements as being representative of mechanisms to place in lathed music containers. With some exceptions, the various movements available are quite similar dimensionally but, obviously, before turning a box or bowl you should check their dimensions. Also, many of the components of the various available movements are similar although not interchangeable. Thus, as I detail components and different aspects of a Reuge movement, this information can be generalized to other movements but the parts cannot be interchanged. You will find, as you become more familiar with the actual musical movements, that they, like the various wood lathes on the market, are frequently a matter of personal choice, availability, and cost.

In general, musical movements are described by the number of tunes they play and also the number of teeth on the comb. For example, I will usually use a Reuge Model 1/18 in most of my lathed music boxes and bowls (Illus. 1-2). This type of movement will play one tune and has eighteen teeth, thus the 1/18. With the exception of the crank-type, the one-tune, eighteen-tooth-comb movement is usually the least expensive. A good rule of thumb, when examining musical movements to use or collect, was stated by L. G. Jaccard: "The more numerous the teeth on the comb, the greater the possibilities of rich music." You will, however, discover very quickly that the more numerous the teeth, the more costly the movement.

Another type of movement that is available and useable in the lathed box is the two-tune, twenty-eight-tooth movement. As you might guess, Reuge

Illus. 1-2 Reuge Model 1/18 Music Movement

refers to this as Model 2/28. Some of the manufacturers produce a one-tune, twenty-eight-tooth movement (1/28). In that these movements are larger than the 1/18 type, the turner must design and plan the turning accordingly. These movements also present the turner with some different problems in designing, if desired, the on/off mechanism.

In general, at least initially, these two types of movements are the ones best suited to use in your lathed music movement containers. I would, however, recommend using the Model 1/18-type movement for your first few boxes or bowls. These movements are usually of good quality and will perform the clockwork sound in a most satisfying manner. Also, the one-tune, eighteen-tooth movement, limits your initial investment. For the various lathed music boxes and bowls presented in later chapters, I have used the Model 1/18 as the movement that is placed in the completed unit.

By way of additional information, the Reuge Model 1/18, with one full winding, will play for three minutes and twenty seconds. The Reuge Model 2/28 will play clockwork music for six minutes, when fully wound. The different length of playing time relates primarily to the size of the movement and the corresponding spring mechanism that is used. The larger movements, as you would assume, have more spring capacity and thus can play longer. With a few exceptions, most available movements are key-wound. Incidentally, the movements should always come with their own key and, in most instances, fixing screws for attaching the movement to the base of the box. As will be discussed, always check the length of the key shaft and the screws, to determine the thickness of the base upon which the movement is mounted. Also, the length of the key shaft will determine how much space is required in the bottom of the box for free movement of the key. (These details will be discussed more fully in later chapters. However, it is worth becoming aware of some of these considerations now as you approach the task of purchasing movements.)

Many other types of winding movements are also available. While you may not want to use them for your lathed musical boxes, it's worth noting them and being aware of their availability. Reuge and a number of manufacturers produce miniature movements that are quite interesting. I have used a number of the Reuge miniature movements in lathed boxes and found them to be fine mechanisms (Illus. 1-3). In that these miniatures are so small, their comb teeth are correspondingly very short and thus produce the tune at a rather high pitch. They're very challenging to the woodturner because they not only require a small box but also an almost paper-thin base upon which the movement is mounted.

Other types of standard winding movements that are available include the Reuge Model 2/22 and Model 2/36. A more sophisticated type of movement produced by Reuge is its changing movement. The standard movements play one or two tunes for each revolution of the cylinder, de-

pending on the model. The changing movements, however, are pinned differently and their comb teeth are separated to allow certain pins to pass between them. To play the different tunes, the entire cylinder, via a release mechanism, is moved laterally to different fixed positions. At each position the movement plays a different tune. Reuge has available an entire series of changing movements beginning with a model CH (changing) 2/28 through a model CH 3/72. As you might guess, these movements are rather expensive, but they are exquisite pieces of craftsmanship. Other manufacturers have somewhat similar movements.

You may be interested to know that Reuge and other movement manufacturers also have a series of electric- and battery-operated musical movements. The electric and battery models are mainly available in the standard one-tune movements, but can be purchased in the larger changing-movement design. The basic design of these types of units is essentially the same as the standard spring-powered movements.

Most movement manufacturers, including Reuge, also produce an entire series of specialty-type movements, which are designed for everything from toys to banks to rocking chairs for children. While such movements usually are man-

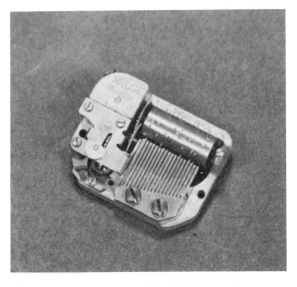

Illus. 1-3 Reuge Model PM 1/18 Music Movement

ufactured with special features, making them adaptable to specific applications, they too use the same component parts as other movements.

One final type of movement that you may logically want to use is the crank-type movement or the manivelle. As detailed in later chapters, the crank movement presents the woodturner with endless design possibilities. There are two basic types of crank movement available. One movement will only permit turning the crank mechanism in one direction. Additionally, this unit generally has the crank shaft and handle extending from the back of the movement. While it is an adequate unit, it does not lend itself to use in most turned boxes. It does, however, present the turner with some interesting possibilities.

The second type of crank movement, at least in the Reuge line, is its Model M 1/18 (Illus. 1-4). As you will note, the crank shaft and handle project from the top of the mechanism. This placement of the crank mechanism gives you a number of options in designing and turning boxes to accommodate it. Also, the mechanism in this unit is designed so that it can be cranked/turned in either direction. As indicated earlier, the crank movements are usually less expensive than the key-wound movements.

Illus. 1-4 Reuge Model M 1/18 Music Movement

One of the significant developments in the music box industry in recent years has been the explosion of available tunes. This is especially true with the 1/18 models currently available. While some of the tunes are difficult to categorize, in general, they tend to fall into four different categories: classical, semiclassical, popular, and modern tunes. In addition to the broad categories, there are religious tunes, Christmas and other seasonal tunes, school tunes, children's tunes, drinking and show tunes. One company (The World of Music Boxes, in Avon, New Jersey) will custom manufacture a movement with any tune you desire if you provide the sheet music.

The larger movements that play two or more selections are usually more limited in their tune offerings. In most instances the larger movements are available in either classical, semiclassical, or very successful popular tunes. Frequently the tune offerings on the larger movements will be by the same composer or of a similar type of music.

The manivelle or crank-type movement is also limited to a very few selections. Most manufacturers tend to have them available only in children's tunes, but a number of movement manufacturers seem to be including more popular tunes in their crank-movement offerings. On the whole, however, the tune offerings are sadly limited. This is regrettable, as the crank movements are a source of great fun and pleasure for adults.

A tradition that dates back to about 1820 is the attachment to the completed musical box of a "tune sheet." The tune sheet, initially a very simple label, indicates the musical tune the box plays. Some of the early tune sheets also carried the initials of the manufacturers. As the industry developed, the tune sheets became extremely elaborate and often carried the name of the musical box maker in addition to the tune or tunes.

With some exceptions, most musical box manufacturers include a tune sheet with their movements. Generally, the tune sheet is affixed to the bottom of the box in the key-winding area. The sheets today are not only informative but they add a nice touch to the completed box.

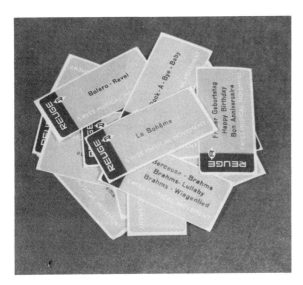

Illus. 1-5 Reuge Tunesheets

It is worth noting that movements from other manufacturers have different dimensions for their bedplates. In planning your turnings, check the bedplate specifications, a rule that also applies to the larger movements that are available.

Illus. 1-6 Reuge Model 1/18 Bedplate

Parts and Specifications

While the major components of music movements and their function were given earlier, more specific information on the various parts needs detailing. A working knowledge of the movements is necessary both to understand how they operate and to assist you in planning for turning musical boxes. In that you will no doubt be using the smaller movements initially in your lathed containers, our discussion will focus on the Model 1/18. Included also will be information on the crank-type movement. The pictured component parts are from Reuge movements.

Illus. 1-6 pictures the typical bedplate of a one-tune, eighteen-tooth movement. You will note the various holes designed to receive the component parts of the movement. Also, the bedplate has three threaded holes for penetration of the fixing screws in attaching the unit to the base of the box. In the Reuge movement, the bedplate is 51 mm long and 43 mm wide. These specifications necessitate an area at least 2¼″ in diameter in a box or bowl to house the movement comfortably. I generally allow a minimum of 2½″ as a diameter for the movement area.

A second major part that affects the dimensions of the lathed box is the movement's governor (Illus. 1-7). The bracket on most movements is that part of the unit that represents its highest point. On the Reuge movement the bracket and jewel plate extends 16 mm from the surface of the bedplate. With the added thickness of the bedplate, the height is roughly 20 mm. It's worth not-

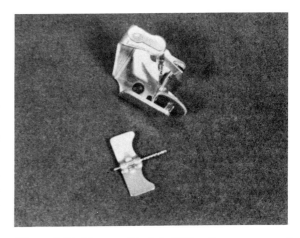

Illus. 1-7 Reuge Model 1/18 Governor and Flywheel with Worm Screw

ing that the dimensions reported are my own that emerged from the initial lathed music box design that housed a Reuge movement. They are, however, sufficiently accurate to meet the needs of the turner.

In that the bracket and bedplate are approximately 20 mm, I usually allow a minimum of ⅞″ as the depth of the area in the box or bowl that will hold the movement. In most instances, when sufficient wood is available in the block, I turn the area to a depth of 1″ as the minimum. Pictured with the governor is the flywheel and the attached endless screw.

The spring housing does not by itself affect specifications for turning boxes, but the threaded winding shaft it contains does (Illus. 1-8). As pictured, the winding shaft of a Reuge model 1/18 extends almost 6 mm from the base of the housing.

Illus. 1-9 Cutaway of Music Box Movement Winding Shaft

Illus. 1-8 Reuge Model 1/18 Spring Barrel Housing: Top and Bottom View

This length must be accounted for in determining the thickness of the sounding board. As a rule, I plan for a sounding board thickness of no more than ¼″. I drill a ⅜″ hole in the sounding board for the winding shaft to protrude through. The winding shaft does not have to penetrate all the way through the sounding board thickness; the reason is that the key for the movement has a threaded internal neck into which the winding shaft screws. Illus. 1-9 pictures a cutaway of a box

showing the winding shaft penetrating a sounding board but without the key. The following picture (Illus. 1-10) demonstrates the winding shaft with the key screwed on it. The dimensional issues presented by the winding shaft must be considered carefully in planning the lathed container for music movements.

Illus. 1-10 Cutaway of Music Box Movement Winding Key

Illus. 1-11 Fixing Screws and Winding Keys

Illus. 1-12 Music Movement Cylinder (1/18)

Illus. 1-13 Music Movement Comb (1/18)

Illus. 1-11 shows the fixing screws and winding keys with necks or shafts of varying lengths. The fixing screws, at least with the Reuge 1/18, should be at least 10 or 12 mm in length for use on a ¼″ sounding base. They are usually available in varying lengths or can be obtained from most hardware stores. While three fixing screws are normally provided with movements when ordered, two are often sufficient to adequately secure the unit to the sounding board.

The key and the length of its shaft are, as indicated earlier, critical variables to account for in planning the music box. With a ¼″ sounding board and a 6-mm winding shaft, I generally use winding keys that have a total length of 10 or 12 mm. If the base area that houses the winding key is at least ½″ deep, there is sufficient clearance for free movement of the key as it unwinds. The issue of key length needs to be anticipated, especially with other movements that you may plan to use. Be certain to verify the specifications before you begin turning. A lathed box or bowl can be made for any movement as long as the specifications of the unit are carefully monitored.

The cylinder with its pins (Illus. 1-12) is approximately 27 mm long. This length includes the shaft that is encased by the cylinder. As the photo indicates, the great wheel is affixed to the cylinder, whose diameter, excluding the pins, approximates 13 mm. As already explained, each cylinder is pinned according to the tune it is supposed to play. In the Reuge movements, each cylinder is marked numerically to indicate the tune it is pinned to play. The comb is also manufactured and marked numerically to correspond with the cylinder tune.

The comb (Illus. 1-13) is 24 mm long and 20 mm wide in the 1/18 movement. As pictured, the two holes are for the comb screws that attach it to the comb base on the bedplate. For proper alignment of the teeth with the cylinder pins these two screws are loosened. Unless you are familiar with procedures for realignment, do not loosen these screws. The varying lengths and thicknesses of the teeth should also be noted. The longer and

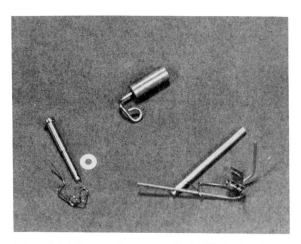

Illus. 1-14 Reuge Stoppers: On/Off Mechanisms

users and collectors prefer to wind the movement and allow it to play itself through without interruption.

An example of an integrated, standard on/off mechanism is the push-pull device pictured in Illus. 1-15. This mechanism projects into the base area of the music box along with the key. The side view of the mechanism indicates its placement in relation to other components of the movement. A spring that attaches to a comb screw is threaded through the shaft and moves into and away from the flywheel as the device is pushed up and pulled down.

wider teeth, as with the tuning fork, are for the bass notes. The shorter and narrower ones are for the treble sounds.

Illus. 1-14 presents three standard on/off mechanisms that can be used with Reuge movements. There are any number of other devices that have been developed to control the playing of the movement. In many instances the turner may decide to devise his or her own on/off mechanisms; some effective options that I developed are presented in later chapters. Also, musical movements do not necessarily require on/off mechanisms. Many

Illus. 1-16 Reuge Movement with Stopper (P717)

Another example of a standard on/off device is depicted in Illus. 1-16. It is designated as a Reuge 717 stopper. The device is a round weight that slides into and away from the flywheel, sliding on a wire that is attached to a comb screw. To activitate the device, and thus the musical movement, the entire box must be tipped to one side or the other. I usually will use this type of stopper in music boxes and bowls that are covered with a glass insert. It is, however, not mandatory for musical containers.

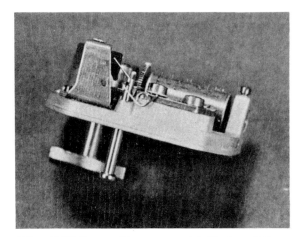

Illus. 1-15 Reuge Movement with Push-pull Stopper: Side View

Part of the fun in working with lathed containers and movements is the never-ending opportunity to problem-solve different design issues that arise. That of on/off mechanisms is one that can be especially tantalizing. I would encourage you to attempt to develop your own devices, if desired, for controlling the movements.

In that you may decide to turn manivelle or crank-type musical boxes, a few details about the Reuge M 1/18 are necessary (Illus. 1-17). The movement is 40 mm high, measuring from the bottom of the bedplate to the top of the crankshaft. Other dimensions of the movement are 45 mm × 40 mm. The comb and the cylinder are slightly larger than on the winding movements. As you will note, the threaded crank handle screws on the threaded shaft. The movement will only play when cranked but, one advantage, it can be cranked in both directions.

The foregoing highlights some of the questions of specifications, parts and related concerns when working with musical movements. It is important to remember that there is no standardization among movement manufacturers, thus the need to check dimensions carefully prior to turning. The use of metric specifications is deliberate. It is intended to initiate you into the domain of the music movement craftsmen. Also, metric dimensions can be extremely useful in the planning and turning of your musical boxes and bowls.

Minor Repairs and Maintenance

Musical movements, while visually fragile, in fact are rather durable. This is especially true of current Swiss movements. The greatest peril for most spring-wound movements is overwinding by the user. Moisture and dust can also endanger the smooth functioning of the movement. However, with appropriate care and occasional minor maintenance, the movements will provide years of service.

When a movement does fail, some suppliers provide either repair service or, in some instances, replacement parts. Parts that generally need repair or replacement are the spring barrel, the governor, or the flywheel and its endless screw. Clearly the spring housed in the barrel is most subject to abuse and thus requires replacement. Unfortunately, because of the initial low cost of the 1/18-type movements, many suppliers do not bother to make replacement parts available. Normally, when a movement fails as the result of a part wearing out, you are best advised to replace the entire movement.

Prior to replacement, with the exception of a broken spring or part, there are a number of minor repairs that can be attempted. An excellent resource on repairing musical movements, especially the larger ones, is Graham Webb's book *The Cylinder Musical Box Handbook*. While Webb focuses on repairing the older and more sophisticated collector's movements, many of his repair suggestions can be applied to smaller movements.

A frequent problem, especially with movements that are exposed, is the gathering of dust, hair, or other debris on the gears or endless screw. When a

Illus. 1-17 Reuge Model M 1/18 and Crank

movement can be wound but will not run, check for things that may be blocking the gears. A common occurrence is for hairs or tiny fabric threads to wind themselves around the endless screw, or even a gear. If available, use a small tweezers to remove such items. Usually this will allow the movement to run again properly.

On occasion, usually from careless handling, the flywheel with its endless screw will come loose from the governor bracket. Unless the bracket has been severcly bent or the flywheel or endless screw damaged, the unit can easily be reassembled. Look under the governor bracket, directly below the jewel plate, and note a small hole. Directly below it, on the base of the governor, is another small hole. These are the two holes that hold the endless screw and the flywheel in place. Place the geared end of the screw in the bottom hole; then, using a finger, carefully lift the governor bracket upward and slide the top of the endless screw in the other hole. The bracket metal, while thick, will allow this procedure. The endless screw and the small gear will usually re-engage themselves.

If on/off devices are used that will attach to the comb screws, care must be exercised when loosening one of the screws. The comb teeth and the cylinder pins are placed in perfect alignment at the factory. The alignment can be disrupted if, when a comb screw is loosened, the comb is accidentally moved. The end result will be musical chaos when the movement begins to play. As a general rule, do not loosen both comb screws at the same time. If it is necessary to loosen one for use with an on/off stopper, check to be certain that the other screw is snug and is firmly holding the comb in place. The teeth and pins can be re-aligned, but normally it takes a trained repairman.

It is important to remember that musical movements are designed and crafted with a reasonable degree of precision and are best treated with care. Some seemingly minor repairs do, in fact, require a measure of expertise and information not generally available to the average user.

With the exception of an occasional oiling, musical movements require a minimum of maintenance. Usually dust and moisture, as suggested, are the greatest enemies of the movement, next to the overzealous winder. Good preventive maintenance is to take care that the movement is not exposed to excessive moisture or humidity. An occasional blowing over the movement, to remove dust and other particles, represents further preventive maintenance. While many movements are totally encased, they still, on occasion, require such care.

As a rule, I oil a movement just before placing it into a musical box or bowl. Illus. 1-18 presents a sketch of oiling points on a 1/18 movement. Either jewelers oil or sewing machine oil should be used on movements. To target the oil more accurately and also to avoid overoiling, I use an opened-paper-clip wire to place a drop on the appropriate spot. Periodically the movement should be oiled for good maintenance of the moving parts.

Over a period of time the brass surfaces of a number of movement components tend to tarnish. If desired, the surfaces can be cleaned with any number of paste cleaners on the market. If cleaning is attempted, approach the task very carefully so as to avoid damaging or clogging moving parts.

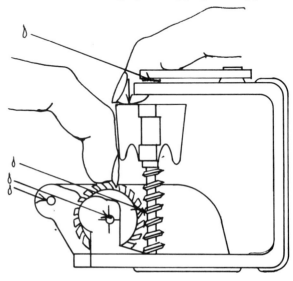

Illus. 1-18 Diagram of Oiling Points on Small Movements

The Woods: Hard and Soft

Preliminaries

While wood is the medium of the turner, it is the tree that makes it all possible. In an age of selective scarcity of many fine woods, the greater tragedy is the continuing depletion of certain species of trees. The pleasure and satisfaction I find in wood is increasingly tempered by this reality. While I am a small consumer of wood, as a collective group individuals may indeed be contributing to the spoiling of our forests.

As with most woodturners, I'm inclined to assume that the lumber yards and sawmills have an endless supply of trees to meet my wood needs. Having a consumer mentality, I am disturbed when they happen to be out of the product that I need at the moment. I rarely think of the complexity of natural production and the implications of my persistent consumer demands.

Prior to an examination of the various woods for turning, some instruction about trees in general seems important. It is imperative that users and enjoyers of wood develop and maintain a measure of enlightenment and awe with respect to its production. Also we must understand the implications of our pleasures and grudgingly protect the sources that make them possible.

Trees, according to Herbert L. Edlin, are large land plants that seek to develop, through the growth process, a central woody stem. This stem- or wood-formation process is what distinguishes trees from the other plants. It is what makes possible the turning block and the lumber for houses. It is important to remember that trees and their total growth process determine not only the quality of our lives but life itself [Petrides, 1973].

To allow for the growth process from seed to sapling to tree, an incredibly complex root system is mandatory. Through an interactive process between the roots and leaves, sap is passed along by a thin layer called the bast or phloem. This layer, also called the inner bark, lies just beneath the actual bark of the tree. The outer bark not only protects the tree from disease, fire, and insects, it also serves to hold moisture in the tree. This point is worth noting for those who plan to dry their own wood. A curiosity about bark is that it has lenticels or small pores that allow the trunk of the tree to breathe [Edlin, 1978].

In examining a cross section of a log, inevitably most persons begin counting the growth rings to determine the age of the tree. These rings are the result of the workings of the cambium of the tree. During the growing season, the cambium makes cells that form the bast or inner bark of the tree [Edlin, 1978]. Simultaneously, it also generates cells, called wood cells, that become the sapwood of the tree [Kozlowski, 1971].

The sapwood, as its name implies, is the carrier of the sap. It also stores sap, in some trees, to enable the tree to produce leaves in the spring. Over a period of time, the inner portion of the sapwood stops participating in the growth process and becomes the heartwood [Edlin, 1978]. It is the heartwood, of course, that is the woodworker's delight.

In most trees, the heartwood develops through a series of chemical changes. The heartwood becomes increasingly hard because its primary function is to support the tree [Edlin, 1978]. It also becomes darker in color and, for all practical purposes, is dead in terms of the growth of the tree. Lest we forget, at the center of the heartwood is the pith. While a disappointment when found in a board, the pith made the tree possible because it is the remains of the sapling, the first growth.

Some Basic Distinctions

In general, most persons separate woods into two primary and rather misleading categories: the hardwoods and the softwoods. The terms are misleading because they are usually interpreted as having reference only to the actual hardness or softness of the wood. In reality, the distinctions are not quite that simple.

The actual differences between hardwood and softwood have to do with the nature and type of cells in a particular tree. While something of a technical discussion is necessary to totally detail the differences, our purposes require only a bit more information. I would, however, urge you to pursue in greater depth the many fascinating phenomena of trees discussed in the various references at the end of this chapter.

Botanists, in classifying trees, identify several families of the plant. Of interest to us are the broad-leaved trees, also called deciduous: those that shed their leaves annually.

The nature of the deciduous trees and how they function results in an extremely complex and efficient cell or pore system. The cell system is particularly complex in the sapwood of the trees. It is the sapwood that must, via its cell system, store sufficient sap for leaf development in the spring. To assist in carrying nourishment for development of the leaf system, the hardwoods also have a highly developed medullary ray cell system. The medullary ray cells radiate out from the center of the tree [Feirer, 1970]. These are the rays that are so conspicuous in a piece of quartersawed oak, and it is the various and different cells that determine what is called the grain of the wood.

As a result of the character and complexity of the cells or pores of deciduous trees, they are generally producers of very durable, frequently dense, and close-grained woods [Kozlowski, 1971]. The nature of their cells makes the wood less likely to splinter. Also, their complex chemical processes result in a wide variety of colors and textures in their woods.

The softwoods or, more appropriately, the conifers produce and maintain a less developed and significantly simpler cell system than the hardwoods [Kozlowski, 1971]. In that their leaves or needles are generally smaller, thicker, coated with a waxy-type substance and thus more resistant to water loss, the conifers require a less complex cell system [Edlin, 1969]. Their moisture needs from the roots are less intense than those of hardwoods because their leaves transpire less [Edlin, 1969]. Softwoods, unlike the hardwoods, also produce and retain resins for their sustenance. The simplicity of their cell structure generally results in wood that is less dense, easier to work but more inclined to splinter, and often loaded with sap.

The preceding presents, in summary fashion, some of the technical distinctions between hardwoods and softwoods. I hope it's sufficient to whet your appetite for more. I have found that the more informed I have become about the complex life process of trees, the more enjoyment I find in working wood. Also, in a practical way, this kind of information is very helpful in both the selection and use of the various woods.

I have also found that an informed awareness assists me greatly when selecting and preparing a block for turning. I find myself focusing more on how I can maximize the natural beauty of the wood rather than on the object that needs to be turned. For those of us who are not especially creative or artistic, the wood itself, if permitted, will often suggest how it should be used. This process, however, assumes that you have an informed sense of what a tree is, how it grows, and what are its life stresses, and then taking the time to study the wood to be used.

Woods for Musical Boxes

It is my good fortune to live in an area of the Midwest that is endowed with hardwood forests. Also, close proximity to lumber dealers and what are called "peckerwood sawmills" makes this area of Illinois something of a woodturner's paradise. A peckerwood sawmill is a small operation that harvests and mills lumber from local farmland and area forests. In most instances they are privately owned, employ only a few people, are nonautomated, and cut lumber primarily for local consumption. More about this type of mill later. While it is advantageous to have such accessibility to material, it is certainly not mandatory; almost all areas produce woods that are useable for woodturning. Additionally, there are numerous mail order suppliers that can provide all types of woods to meet the turner's needs.

As noted earlier, craftsmen engaged in making musical boxes in the 19th century tended to avoid certain woods. It was their belief that some woods, oak being one, would mute or deaden the musical sounds created by the movement. While they used pine, most of their boxes were crafted from the denser hardwoods. To date, this has not been my experience. I have used woods that are less effective carriers of vibrations from the movements. The degree of variance, however, has been slight and hardly noticeable. In part, the matter of volume may relate as much to the movement itself as to the wood that encloses it. Part of the fun in turning musical boxes is the experimentation with different woods and movements.

Before discussing woods that I have used in turning musical boxes and bowls, some information about the hardwoods seems in order. For example, when you purchase hardwoods you will be obtaining either kiln dried (KN) or air dried (AD) lumber. There are, thus, two different methods of removing moisture from lumber. As a general rule, the KD material is more expensive because of the use of the kiln process. Most furniture makers and professional craftsmen alike will only use kiln dried material and gladly pay the extra cost. The kiln process removes the moisture more uniformly and thoroughly, so the wood is more stable and less likely to warp or check.

Many craftsmen, however, prefer air dried material. Hardwoods purchased at the peckerwood mills (and from some suppliers) are usually air dried. Not only is it generally less expensive but it is also something the craftsperson can do on his or her own. Most woodworkers have a stash of lumber somewhere in the shop or attic that they're allowing to dry for a period of years. The grain ends have been coated with all types of substances to allow for a slow and more uniform drying. When ready, it's an immense pleasure to pull out and work a board or a block that you have been drying for a period of years. A number of books in the bibliography provide specific suggestions on how to prepare and dry your own wood.

In addition to KD and AD lumber, you can also use green wood for turning. Green wood is a delight to turn. However, it must be processed according to a number of techniques or it will split and check. Dale Nish has a superb book, *Artistic Woodturning*, that discusses in detail the "harvesting" and preparation of green woods for turning. Other authors suggest techniques that include the use of standard kitchen or microwave ovens. The use of the chemical polyethylene glycol (PEG) gives the woodturner another method of preparing green wood for turning. Patrick Spielman's book *Working Green Wood with PEG* is an excellent resource for using this chemical process.

Hardwood lumber grading is another area where some knowledge can be useful. Both the softwood and hardwood lumber industries have developed very specific methods and techniques for grading the quality of lumber. While there are some similarities in the two systems, hardwood lumber grading is a substantially more sophisticated process. For most woodworkers, a general working knowledge of the various hardwood grades is all that is necessary. References that present both methods are included in the bibliography for this chapter. A more effective way to learn the grading system, especially with reference to the hardwoods, is to ask an informed dealer to explain it. You will quickly discover the differences when you ask the price of FAS (firsts and seconds: the best grades of hardwood) and select, or lower grades. Price can be an excellent motivator in learning and understanding the grading system.

Another bit of information that is helpful is the way measurements are used in describing the hardwoods. As with the softwoods, the primary unit of measurement is the board foot. This unit, by the way, is also the basis for pricing most lumber. Thickness of hardwoods is generally stated in terms of quarter-inch intervals. For example, a 1"-thick hardwood board would be described as being 4/4's (four-quarters); a 1¼"-thick board would be

5/4's (five-quarters) and so on. These thicknesses are usually the rough, unsurfaced dimensions. Frequently you will encounter hardwoods referred to as being S2S. This reference simply means that the board has been surfaced (planed) on two sides. The surfacing process obviously reduces the thickness of the board; it also raises the price. You must allow for this reduction from nominal size to actual surfaced size when planning for an exact project.

Widths are generally unpredictable in the hardwoods because of the necessity to maximize the log when sawing. This lack of consistency also applies to length. Frequently mills or dealers will trim boards to length. That, however, only adds more to the cost of the material. It does make the material easier to handle and, in many instances, more marketable. As an aside, I seldom buy hardwoods that have been surfaced or cut to length. This not only saves on the cost of lumber but leaves a thicker board. In turning musical boxes, an additional fraction of an inch in thickness can often determine whether or not a particular piece of wood can be used.

When selecting hardwoods from a dealer for music boxes or bowls, I'm inclined to the unusual or the seemingly unuseable piece. Most of the pieces I prefer to use for turning are the cutoffs from a lumber dealer or mill. In point of fact, my preference for wood is usually for those pieces that others would consider worthless. I look for pieces that contain chaotic and totally unpredictable grains. Incidentally, the grain of the wood is determined by the cell structure in a particular species of tree. Figure, another term that is used in describing a hardwood board, relates to the many and diverse patterns that you see in the wood. The figure is primarily the result of the different life stresses and growth processes of the tree. Also, figure can be the result of how the log was sawed and, in many instances, from what part of the tree the wood came.

I try to find, for example, crotch wood, where the grain tends to run in a series of directions. In walnut, I look for what is sometimes called "satin-wood," a figure that gives the wood a three-dimensional effect. Areas with knots or rot also get my attention, along with edges still covered with bark. Insect damage, fire scorches, areas that held nails, holes and scars are other "defects" that I look for in material. In short, I try to find the unusual, the different which, in many instances, is also the least expensive. More about this shortly.

In general, selection of wood to use for turning should be a very personal process. For me, the actual rummaging through a stack of hardwood is nothing less than total pleasure. My addiction to wood is so complete that I examine and enjoy each board even though I have no intention of buying it. While I generally know the type and amount of material I need prior to going to a dealer, the actual piece or pieces I want to discover on my own. I want to select the board that pleases me regardless of what the dealer may think. Most dealers, within limits, allow this process of sorting and selecting your own material. They frequently will forklift-down stacks for you to go through. If they are not helpful, then find another supplier. These privileges do, however, necessitate not only the careful handling of the stock but also putting the piles back in order when finished.

Hardwoods that I use in music box or bowl turning must frequently be purchased from either local dealers or mail order suppliers. For some time I have been using bocote (cordia) for musical boxes. In that bocote is an imported wood, at least the type I use, it is generally only available through a dealer or supplier. While quite expensive, it is well worth the price. Bocote is a very attractive and dense wood that quickly dulls turning tools but finishes exquisitely. Because of its cost, I use it only in small music box designs. The scraps make excellent and very different decorative plugs for use in boxes, bowls, or lids.

In addition to oak and walnut, I also purchase Honduran mahogany from a local hardwood dealer. While an import and rather expensive, it is an excellent turning wood for musical boxes. In that mahogany darkens with age and becomes even more attractive, I usually will cut turning blocks and lids and let them sit exposed to the air for a period of months before using. While it is an extremely soft wood, mahogany makes an attractive lathed musical box. Normally I purchase 4/4's for lids and 6/4's or 8/4's for the boxes.

When available, I usually purchase a number of the imported reddish woods. Specifically, I use padouk, vermillion, and bubinga. I refer to all these woods as reddish in color even though bubinga is somewhat darker and laced with traces of black. In that all three are very expensive, I will sometimes limit their use to a lid or knob while the actual music box is turned from another wood. Also, these woods are difficult to obtain in thicknesses generally required in turning musical boxes or bowls. The scraps, by the way, are excellent for use as plugs in lids and boxes and bowls.

There are, as you will discover, an almost endless array of other woods, both foreign and domestic, that are available from local dealers and mail order suppliers. On occasion I will buy or order a small quantity of something exotic or different just to try it. It's not only fun; it also adds to my knowledge of the different trees and woods from around the world.

One word of caution. A number of the hardwoods, expecially some imports, may be toxic and must be handled with care. Usually the sawdust of these woods is the problem. You would be wise to check on the possible toxicity of any wood that you plan to work with over a period of time. Also many woods, both domestic and foreign, can cause skin irritations or nasal and bronchial reactions. Some are prone to cause allergic reactions in most persons who use them. It goes without saying that the woodturner should, especially with a wood never used before, wear a dust mask and gloves. If your dealer or supplier is not knowledgeable about the toxic or allergic qualities of woods purchased, information can usually be obtained by writing to U.S. Department of Agriculture, Forest Products Laboratory, Box 5130, Madison, WI 53705. Also, a number of references listed in the bibliography discuss toxicity and allergic factors in wood.

A final dealer-type wood that I use in some music boxes is pine. In general, I use contruction 2-by-4's and #3 Common construction grade boards. As will be discussed, I use pine in some crank-type (manivelle) music boxes. Also, for new designs, I use pine as the material for crafting a prototype box or bowl. It's sufficiently inexpensive and easy to work with that it lends itself to use in designing and turning new projects. Pine is also a good choice of wood for the beginning turner to practice with and develop turning skills. It's also worth having pine in the shop for use as glue blocks for some types of faceplate turning.

As mentioned earlier, I frequently obtain hardwoods for turning musical boxes or bowls from peckerwood sawmills. While the material is almost always air dried (AD), it normally has been stacked out of the weather for a number of years. Rarely have I had a problem with air dried hardwoods in turning. There are a number of distinct advantages to the sawmills as a source of hardwoods, even though the wood is not kiln dried (KD). One major advantage, as mentioned earlier, is price. While high-quality grades are usually available, most of the material is the lower-grade hardwoods. This makes the cost even more attractive, especially for stock for woodturning.

Another advantage of the sawmill, when one is available, is that the lower grades of hardwoods are generally sawed in thicker dimensions. For example, I frequently buy walnut that is 20/4's and 24/4's thick and, within limits, as wide as desired. These thicknesses are a woodturner's dream for turning large bowls and other pieces. Also, the lower-grade hardwoods have, I believe, more character than the better grades. The woods are generally more colorful with exotic graining and unusual figure. Frequently the knots and crotch grain are in the stock along with a whole series of other aberrations from tree growth. Oftentimes there are portions of rot, fire damage, insect infestation remains, metal staining from old nails, bark and other oddities not found in the better grades of wood. It is precisely the kind of material that I prefer for woodturning.

Peckerwood mills also have local hardwoods that are not usually handled by dealers. For example, one mill where I purchase lumber has osage orange—or the more common name, hedge—on a regular basis. Hedge is one of the denser woods and has a beautiful yellow color to it. It's a superb wood to finish but very difficult to turn because of its hardness. I have also been able to obtain hedge fence posts that are well over sixty years old from a mill. Many of my more interesting (in my opinion) musical boxes and bowls are turned from osage. A number of these pieces are pictured in other sections of the book. Also, turning a musical bowl from a hedge fence post is detailed in Chapter 7.

Another local wood that is available is American hackberry. While it is not an especially attractive hardwood, it is excellent for making handles for turning tools. Shagbark hickory is also available and I sometimes will use it for handles. My current preference, however, is hackberry, which makes an excellent nonslip handle.

A rather unusual wood that I've been able to obtain from sawmills and use in music boxes and bowls is spalted sycamore. Spalting, as you may know, results from the rotting process of the wood. The primary causes of spalting seem to be a combination of moisture, fungus, and air. Spalting is not found in all trees but is often found in maple, beech, elm, and sycamore. Frequently the mills will discard the "rotten" wood or grind it up with other milling debris. The spalted woods are a bit problematical to turn and finish but they make for a unique piece when completed. In the sections dealing with specifics of turning music boxes, one example presented uses spalted sycamore.

A number of other local hardwoods that I've used in musical boxes are persimmon, sassafras, and black cherry. These are also available at peckerwood mills in this area and are all excellent for turning music boxes or bowls. I use a great deal of cherry, both AD and KD, in turning musical containers. For the beginning turner, persimmon is a delightful wood with which to develop turning skills. Using either cutting or scraping methods, you can almost always create large curly shavings and have a sense of doing things right. Sassafras, while rather soft and smelly, is an excellent and very durable wood for turned pieces. It does not, however, finish well. There are a multitude of other woods that I have tried that, in many instances, can be obtained at local mills. Those mentioned are but a few of the many that can be used in turning musical containers.

Burls can also be obtained from sawmills. Very often they are chainsawed off the logs and discarded as being of no value. Frequently you will find them on a firewood pile or discarded around the mill area. While some burls are hollow and of

Illus. 1-19 Walnut Turning Stock

Illus. 1-20 Osage Orange (Hedge)
Blocks for Turning

Illus. 1-21 Split Spalted Sycamore Log

Illus. 1-22 Burls

Illus. 1-23 Cherry Crotch Wood from Woodpile

little value for turning, when you find a solid one you will be amazed at the treasure you have found when you begin to turn it. Burls are truly unique pieces in terms of grain and color. Be sure you approach them as green wood, because very often they are saturated with water from laying out in the open.

As stated earlier, my home locale is fortunate with respect to the availability of both woods and sawmills. With some initiative you may very well discover peckerwood or similar mills in your own part of the country. Usually the operations are about the same; only the woods are different, and that's what it's all about.

In addition to woods from dealers and sawmills, I also use materials from both my own and others' backyard wood piles. Other sources of wood for turning music boxes are clearing activities for new construction and tree trimming by city departments or power companies. Much of my oak and cherry, especially crotch wood, comes from these sources. Since I have chainsaws, that greatly sim-

plifies the task both of cutting logs to size and also of checking on their value for turning.

Frequently material obtained this way must be handled as green wood. Often, however, especially from a covered wood pile, the material is sufficiently dry for immediate use. You can pretty well tell the extent of moisture by feeling and smelling the actual wood and also by examining the bark, both outer and inner. A number of references for this chapter detail some of the specifics on these and other procedures in handling wood from these sources.

As you become aware of the multiple sources of wood that are available at no cost, you will discover an endless supply of fascinating materials for turning. While some of these sources may not be sufficient or adequate for the professional turner, for the hobbyist they are more than adequate. Also, my experience suggests that the turned pieces that I enjoy the most are from wood that I found and nursed to readiness. I'm confident your experience will be the same.

References

Music Movements

Bowers, Q. David, *Encyclopedia of Automatic Musical Instruments*. Vestal, NY: Vestal Press, 1972.
————, ed., *A Guidebook of Automatic Musical Instruments*, vols. 1 and 2. Vestal, NY: Vestal Press, 1968.

"Brief History of Reuge, S.A." Author's correspondence with Reuge, S.A., Ste.-Croix, Switzerland.

Buchner, Alexander, *Mechanical Musical Instruments*, transl. Iris Urwin. London: Batchworth, 1959.

Chapuis, Alfred, *History of the Musical Box and of Mechanical Music*, Eng. transl., J.E. Roesch; eds., H.M. and H.F. Fitch. Summit, NJ: Musical Box Society, International, 1980.

Clark, John E.T., *Musical Boxes: A History and Appreciation*. London: Allen & Unwin, 1961.

Dearling, Robert, and Celia Rust Brian, *The Guinness Book of Music Facts*. Middlesex, England: Guinness Superlatives, 1976.

de Waard, Romke, *From Music Boxes to Street Organs*. Vestal, NY: Vestal Press, 1962.

Hoke, Helen, and John Hoke, *Music Boxes, Their Lore and Lure*. NY: Hawthorn Books, 1957.

Jaccard, L.G., *Origin and Development of the Music Box*. Musical Box Society, International, 1967. (*Hobbies* Magazine, 1938)

Mosoriak, Roy, *The Curious History of Music Boxes*. Chicago: Lightner Publishing Co., 1943.

Ord-Hume, Arthur W.J.G., *Clock-Work Music: An Illustrated History of Mechanical Musical Instruments*. NY: Crown, 1973.
————, *Musical Box: A History and Collectors Guide*. London: Allen & Unwin, 1980.

Webb, Graham, *The Cylinder Musical Box Handbook*. London: Faber & Faber, 1968.

(Organization: Musical Box Society, International, Box 205, Rte. 3, Morgantown, IN 46160)

Wood

Baker, Glen E., and L. Dayle Yeager, *Wood Technology*. Indianapolis: Howard W. Sams, 1974.

Coleman, Donald G., *Woodworking Factbook*. NY: Robert Speller, 1966.

Constantine, Albert, *Know Your Woods*, rev. Harry J. Hobbs. NY: Charles Scribner's Sons, 1975.

Corner, E.J.H. *The Life of Plants*. Chicago: Univ. of Chicago Press, 1964.

Edlin, Herbert L., *What Wood Is That? A Manual of Wood Identification*. NY: Viking, 1969.

Feirer, John L., *Cabinetmaking and Millwork*. Peoria, IL: Chas. A. Bennett, 1970.

Harlow, William M., *Inside Wood: Masterpiece of Nature*. Washington, D.C.: American Forestry Assoc., 1970.

Hoadley, R. Bruce, *Understanding Wood: A Craftsman's Guide to Wood Technology*. Newtown, CT: Taunton Press, 1980.

Jane, F.W., *The Structure of Wood*. London: Adam & Clarks Black, 1956.

Kozlowski, T.T., *Growth and Development of Trees*. NY: Academic Press, 1971.

Kribs, David A., *Commercial Foreign Woods on the American Market*. NY: Dover, 1976.

Lindquist, Mark, "Spalted Wood: Rare Jewels from Death and Decay," *Fine Woodworking*, vol. 2, no. 1 (Summer 1977), Newtown, CT: Taunton Press.

Nakashima, George, *The Soul of a Tree: A Woodworker's Reflections*. NY: Kodansha International, 1981.

Panshin, A.A., and Carl de Zeeuw, *Textbook of Wood Technology*, 4th ed. NY: McGraw-Hill, 1980.

Petrides, George A., *A Field Guide to Trees and Shrubs*. Boston: Houghton Mifflin, 1973.

Spielman, Patrick, *Working Green Wood with PEG*. NY: Sterling, 1981.

Woodturning: The Faceplate Method

Chapter 2

WOODTURNING: THE FACEPLATE METHOD

Woodturning, whether spindle or faceplate, is very much what is called a psychomotor skill. It has to do with eye, hand, and body coordination; it has to do with information, application, and repetition. While some persons may be physically restricted in developing skills in this area, for most, the turning of wood is an achievable task. Also, as with any psychomotor skill, individual differences can affect the level of skill achieved. For most, however, as in many skill areas, our capacity to perform far outweighs our willingness. Through accurate information, the application of some problem-solving skills, and persistent turning, most who approach the lathe can progressively improve their turning skills.

While skill development will emerge through informed and continuous turning, the more desirable goal is to focus on the satisfaction you can obtain from interacting with the lathe, the tools, and the wood. Unless your livelihood depends on it, turning should be for the pleasure and pure enjoyment it brings to the turner.

In general, unlike other tools, the wood lathe is a very forgiving and understanding tool. It encourages and allows for our best but it never chides when our performance is something less. The lathe always permits us to walk away with something, even though it's smaller and shaped differently than we had planned. This tool always allows us to salvage our dignity.

The lathe and turning tools also permit the sharing of emotion. It's a good listener in that, without interruption but with constant involvement, it and the tools allow us to move through a range of emotions. It's tolerant of anger but also receptive to our more creative emotions. The lathe has a way of allowing the turner to be honest.

Woodturning also allows the individual to freely move into a dimension of time that is defined by experiences and not the clock. It's not possible to turn for a few minutes. You can't take the clock into the world of woodturning. Somehow, once that motor begins to hum, you seem to move into another time frame.

As a principle of learning, turning skills will develop or be refined as an outgrowth of persistent and informed use of the tool. The real capacity and function of the lathe and what is called turning, goes beyond simple skill development. However, information is necessary in order to perform a given task, even with the lathe. To that end, it's important that we examine some specific information about woodturning. In addition to the material presented, for more detailed information and assistance in skill development, a bibliography has been provided at the end of the chapter.

Faceplate Turning: An Overview

Turning musical boxes and bowls is essentially the same as turning any other piece. Both employ the use of faceplates and the methods and techniques appropriate to this kind of woodturning. As you will discover, some additional tasks in turning music boxes necessitate some specific procedures that normally are not factors in turning standard bowls. Also, there are some design issues in music box turning that you need to consider more carefully than in standard faceplate turning. These and related issues are addressed very specifically in later chapters that detail procedures for turning musical boxes and bowls.

For those who are experienced turners, the

problems, techniques, and methods of faceplate turning have already been addressed and solved. For the beginning turner, however, faceplate turning may still be somewhat unclear. Thus we first briefly explore in a general way, which overview will then be followed by a more detailed examination of faceplace turning, at least as I do it in relation to music boxes.

There are two basic methods in woodturning: spindle turning and faceplate turning. The faceplate method employs the use of the lathe headstock. Spindle turning uses both the headstock and the tailstock. While spindle turning is traditionally used for crafting such items as table legs and other items of length, mounted between the two stocks, faceplate turning is used for bowls and similar pieces turned only on the headstock.

Faceplate turning on the headstock of the lathe literally employs a threaded metal plate. Usually the plate is 3″ or 6″ in diameter, with holes for screws through the surface. It is this threaded plate, using wood screws, that holds a pre-rounded wooden block on the headstock for turning. Depending on the type of lathe and also the size of the block to be turned, faceplate turning

can be done "in-board" (over the lathe bed) or "out-board" (on the outer side of the headstock).

After the faceplate has been attached to the center of a block with wood screws, the assembly is threaded on the headstock. This is followed by properly aligning the tool rest, and turning can begin. Dependent on the degree of turning experience, personal preference, and tool availability, the turner may use either scrapers, deep gouges, or chisels, or some combination of the three. In most instances the outside of the block is turned to shape first, followed by the turning of the inside if a bowl is planned. Final surface finishing, if necessary, can be accomplished by using a series of different grades of abrasive paper, from coarse to fine, and a final rubbing with extra-fine steel wool.

The finished piece and the faceplate are removed from the headstock and the screws holding the two are removed. The screw holes in the base can be either filled with plastic wood, with plugs, or left open to be covered later with felt. The base of the piece is finished with abrasive papers and then, using oil or surface finishes, the project is complete.

Faceplate Turning: The Process

Preliminaries

With the foregoing overview as a point of reference, I expand on some of the methods of faceplate turning that have been effective for me, focusing, when possible, on their specific application to turning musical boxes and bowls. To begin, I have approximately eight 3″ faceplates that I use not only for turning blocks but also for the various chucks and screw-centers that I make and use. (I will discuss chucks and screw-centers in detail a bit later.) Any number of the faceplates are always unavailable for new turnings because they're attached to one of the chucks or some other partially turned bowl.

On a number of occasions a particular turning

may not be taking shape the way that I had hoped. Either my original design was faulty, the wood may not be cooperating, or I may not be cooperating with the wood. Whatever causes it, I will stop turning and set the block aside, leaving the faceplate attached. By leaving the faceplate attached, this allows me to return another day and begin turning without having to realign the plate and the block. That obviously ties up one of the faceplates.

When I have to turn a lot of items for a sale, I will usually attach blocks to as many faceplates as I can find that are not in use. This allows a more assembly-oriented method of turning. It permits me to remain at the lathe until all the blocks have been turned. When necessary, I will stop to shape

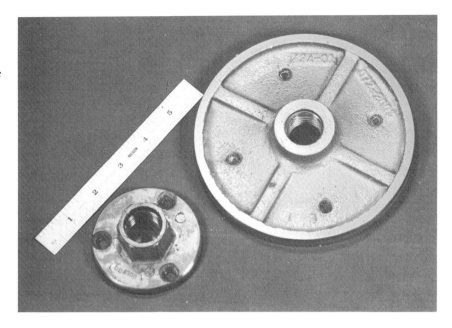

Illus. 2-1 Faceplates:
3″ and 6″

a tool. However, when the initial batch is turned, I will repeat the process. Thus my many faceplates; on occasion I wish I had more. For most turning, including musical boxes, you really only need two faceplates and a bit of flexibility and planning. Incidentally, for turning larger bowls and boxes, I usually use a 6″ faceplate. The larger plate provides greater stability and safety when working with larger blocks. (Illus. 2-1)

Before I discuss using glue blocks in the next section, a few comments on how I attach faceplates are in order. With some exceptions, most of the time I attach the faceplate directly to the block to be turned; with possibly one exception I always use this method in turning music boxes and bowls. As you will note later, the use of chucks allows me to turn out the area where the screws have penetrated the base of the block. In any event, I use either ½″ × 8 or ¾″ × 8 flathead or oval head Phillips wood screws to attach faceplates. The reason I prefer Phillips screws is that I use a variable speed, reversible electric drill with a Phillips bit to insert and remove the screws. The Phillips prevents bit slippage and, also, this type of slot tends to last longer. On occasion, especially with extremely hard woods like bocote or hedge, I use a

Yankee Drill to make pilot holes in the block. This prevents any splitting of the block when the screws are inserted.

Templates, Blocks, and Band Sawing

According to the size of the block required for a particular piece or music box, I always saw the block round prior to mounting it on a faceplate. I try to maximize the wood by seeking to match, for minimum waste, my available stock with the planned turning. When the block diameter needed is 3½″ or less, I use a plastic circle template to pattern the block. The template has a series of twelve circles ranging in diameter from 1½″ to 3½″. Another of its features is that it is premarked for locating the exact center of the circle. I always mark the center when tracing because it simplifies centering the faceplate when attaching it to the block. This type of template is usually available at stationery supply stores.

For larger projects, I make circle patterns with a graduated school compass. The pointed leg marks the center of the block and the pencil patterns the perfect circle for cutting. For some of my standardized music boxes I use a 5″ or 6″ round

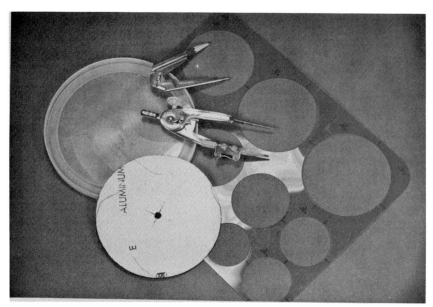

sanding disk to pattern the block. On occasion, plastic coffee can covers have also been used (Illus. 2-2).

After tracing the circles, I saw the block round on the band saw. I try to have a ¼″ × 5 teeth per inch, skip tooth blade in the saw; that width allows the sawing of both smaller-circle blocks and larger ones. I cut the blocks as perfectly round as possible. I have found that a few extra minutes on the band saw eliminates a great deal of unnecessary rough turning on the lathe when the block is not round. After these procedures, I mount the faceplate directly to the block unless the project requires a glue block.

With the exception of spalted woods, I will usually turn nonmusic bowls using round blocks glued to the base of the piece. Spalted woods, because of their rot, often do not hold well with glue. Also, in turning spalted woods, I'm usually very agressive both with the tools and abrasive papers. Thus I usually use screws on this type of wood. All other woods normally can be turned using glue blocks; I don't especially like screw holes, even when they're filled, on the bottom of a nice piece. Using felt dots to cover the holes, though I do it on occasion, is not the best solution

either. While you will find that chucks are an effective alternative to glue blocks when turning music boxes or bowls, you may prefer the gluing process as the best method for your turning.

Since I use pine for other shop projects, I usually have an endless supply of scraps. Using a template, I trace a series of round glue blocks in the pine stock. Normally, for a 3″ faceplate, I try to make them with a diameter of 3½″. I have found that when they're much smaller in diameter, the wood screws, when applying the faceplate, tend to split the pine. When available, I also use 3½″ or larger circles from plywood. I usually cut the circles on the band saw, using a ¼″ blade. After blowing the sawdust off both the pine and the turning block, I'm ready for gluing.

When gluing the blocks I use Elmer's or a similar white glue. If I plan to split the glue block from the finished turned piece, I use a regular piece of paper between the pine and the turning block. I apply glue to one side of the pine circle and smear it around with the paper insert so that the entire face is covered with glue. After placing the piece of paper so that it covers the entire surface, I spread more glue on the top side of the paper. Next I center the glued pine block and paper on the turning block. This is followed by clamping the entire assembly with two Jorgenson bar clamps until dry (Illus. 2-3).

After turning, I split the glue block from the finished piece by using an old but sharp blade from a hand plane. This method of gluing turning blocks is effective, but it leaves an unfinished base that is also covered with dry glue and paper. To simplify removal of this mess, I sand the base of the bowl, or whatever I've turned, on a 6″ × 48″ belt sander using a 40-grit belt. I have a number of old 40-grit belts that are used exclusively for this purpose. The glue, when it becomes hot from friction, will ruin most finer grit belts.

Frequently, using a parting tool, I will remove the pine block from the finished piece as it turns on the lathe. This procedure enables me to tool away most of the glue and paper, and also to obtain a reasonable finish on the bottom of the piece. The method is a bit tricky at first in that, unless you grab the piece by the edge as you make the final cut, it will fly off. If it's an exceptionally fine piece, I usually won't risk it. In those instances, I will stop cutting with the parting tool when ap-proximately ½″ of pine shaft remains, turn off the lathe and, with a hack saw, cut through the re-maining shaft. This leaves only a small area on the base to clean up. Incidentally, for those in a hurry, the glue block and turned piece can be separated using a band saw. Separate the two pieces by plac-ing the entire assembly on its side on the band saw table and cutting at the glue joint.

It may interest you to know that I almost always wear a leather glove on my left hand (I'm right-handed) when turning. I always wear a glove when doing the above procedure, that is, grabbing the rotating bowl as it is parted from the glue block. When using abrasive papers on a piece, I always wear both gloves. After the usual number of finger and knuckle injuries, burns, and splinters, I be-gan wearing rather inexpensive suede gloves. I have found the gloves permit a better grip when removing a stuck faceplate and, in general, are very useful and protective. When turning what I consider a potentially hazardous piece, I will also wear a full-face safety mask. The issue of personal safety has always been a major consideration in my turning, especially faceplate turning. At lathe

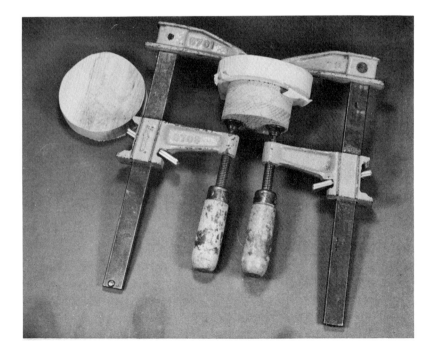

Illus. 2-3 Preparing a Glue Block

speeds, as you may know or will learn, things happen very quickly. I will discuss some safety considerations when I go into turning the centers from square blocks, turning pieces off-center, or lathing blocks from rough hedge fence posts.

In preparing smaller blocks to turn as bowls or containers with lids, I also use 3½″ pine rounds. Rather than using glue, however, I use double-face tape to hold the turning piece and the pine block firmly together. I seldom use this method in turning music boxes, but it is an excellent method for turning many other pieces. Usually I use two strips of 1″-wide tape placed side by side on the pine piece, a bit longer than the diameter of the block to be attached for turning. After removing the material covering the surface of the tape, the turning block is placed firmly on the tape surface in the center of the pine block. I then, very briefly, clamp the assembly together using a bar clamp (Illus. 2-4).

The taping process is followed by the usual faceplate mounting and then the piece is turned. In turning with the tape method, don't be too aggressive with the tools. However, I have found through a number of crude experiments that the tape produces an extremely good bond with the wood and, using normal turning techniques, it holds very well. Initially, you must develop some confidence in the tape and in the reality that it will hold the block in place. The finished piece can be removed from the tape with relative ease and the base of the turning is clean.

Although the foregoing discussion did not focus specifically on faceplate turning musical boxes and bowls, the information is useful in a general way to those interested in this method of turning. Also, on a number of the examples discussed in later chapters, you may choose to use one of the above methods rather than the suggested procedure.

Measurement and Miscellaneous Devices

In faceplate turning, especially with musical boxes or boxes with lids, I find a variety of measuring devices to be critical (Illus. 2-5). While I frequently use the tool I happen to be turning with to obtain a gross indication of depth in the center of a bowl or box, more precise measurements are mandatory. I use a 5″ metal ruler graduated by ⅛″ on one side and a metric scale on the other. I often use the metric system because it's simple and

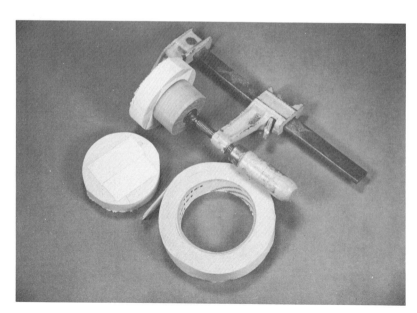

Illus. 2-4 Preparing Turning Blocks with Double-face Tape

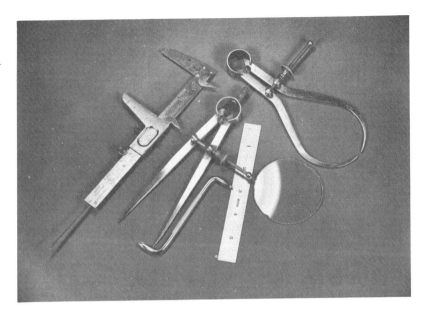

Illus. 2-5 Measuring Devices for Turning

easier to read. The metric system has also proved helpful in that musical movements are manufactured and described via the metric system.

Another device I have found indispensable is a vernier caliper. Its ability to give simultaneous inside/outside measurements is invaluable. I use it more as a specific guide than as an actual measurement device. In later chapters, I demonstrate the usefulness of the caliper in faceplate turning. The vernier caliper and other devices I mention can be obtained with minimal investment if you shop around. There is no need for high-quality measuring devices in faceplate turning.

In addition to the school compass with a pencil for a leg, I also use a metal divider on occasion. Another device I sometimes use to check bowl or box thickness is on outside caliper. Most of the time I can tell the thickness of a bowl by looking at and feeling the wall, but when turning a very thin wall the caliper has been helpful. With my measuring instruments, although not one of them, I keep a small, angled Phillips screwdriver. Frequently, after some aggressive turning, I use this tool to tighten the faceplate screws while the piece is mounted on the lathe.

As you will discover, on some of my music boxes I place a round glass insert inside the box over the musical movement. This permits the user to observe the mechanism. I will discuss the use of glass in those sections dealing with specifics of musical boxes. However, it's worth noting here that I often use one of those glass inserts as a measuring device when turning. I have standardized some of my music boxes to use a $2\frac{3}{4}''$-diameter glass insert. The shoulder that is cut inside the box supports the glass inserts, and I use the insert to check the accuracy of the inside shoulder so that there will be a good fit when the box is completed. Suggestions will be given regarding glass cutting when it's appropriate to one of the musical boxes.

Scraping and Tools

Assuming your faceplate with the turning block is mounted on the lathe, after alignment of the tool rest turning can begin. But before discussing scraping as a turning technique, a few preliminaries are in order. Whether turning the outside or inside of a musical box, I align the tool rest a shade over the midpoint of the block. Normally I have the tool rest placed about one-quarter inch from the piece to be turned. When the block is not reasonably round, or seems off-center, I rotate it to be certain that it will not strike the tool rest when the lathe is on. If the rest is too close, I move it back, rotate the block again, and then reset the rest to one-quarter inch from the piece and begin turning.

With larger blocks I frequently move the tailstock into the block. I have a pointed ball-bearing center in the tailstock that is used for this procedure. The tailstock method is used, in part, for reasons of personal safety. However, this method also supports the faceplate-mounted block very effectively during the turning process. As I'm rather aggressive in roughing out the larger blocks, I can force the faceplate screws loose and thus throw the block off center. I rarely turn outboard, probably for this reason. In any event, the tailstock moved into the piece will prevent the faceplate screws from loosening.

Using a four-inch tool rest, I rough-turn much of the inside of a music box or bowl with the tailstock firmly in place. This procedure is a bit awkward at first but very effective; it eliminates the possibility of a block flying off the faceplate.

In discussing the use of chucks and how they're used in turning musical boxes and lids, I again suggest the use of the tailstock as a support system. When turning the bottom portion of a large music box or bowl, mounted on a wooden chuck, the tailstock method becomes almost mandatory. More about this procedure later.

Unless I'm turning a large, rather rough block, I generally run my lathe at 2220 rpm. With a larger block or some other piece that seems hazardous, I rough-turn the piece at 1475 rpm and then speed up. When I turn a block off-center, which I will later describe, I often drop to 990 rpm. Finishing with abrasive papers is normally done at 2220 rpm.

I do almost all of my faceplate turning using scrapers as tools. While, on occasion, I turn with a three-eighths-inch-deep gouge, I prefer the scraping method. I also use chisels, but rarely as they were designed to be used. This will become

Illus. 2-6 Selected Turning Tools

apparent in the various chapters dealing with the turning of musical boxes and bowls.

When purchasing turning tools, my preference is to obtain ones without handles, and to turn and fit my own handles. I like handles that are rather long and thick (Illus. 2-6). Some of my handles, as previously mentioned, I turn from hickory. Most, however, are turned from hackberry. It's a great deal of fun to design and turn your own tool handles. Using a spear chisel, I make a series of rings on the butt end of the handle: a different series for each tool, thus giving me instant recognition of the tool desired. Incidentally, I finish the handles with Watco Danish Oil.

For rough turning, especially on the larger blocks, I use a 1″ roundnose scraper, pointed slightly downwards. It removes the wood effectively and also allows for some initial shaping of

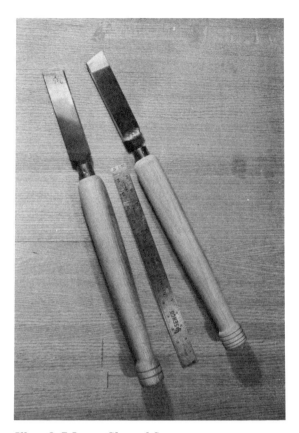

Illus. 2-7 Large Skewed Scrapers

With musical boxes and bowls, it is necessary to turn out a special area where the movement is to be placed. Specifics about this will be discussed in detail later. To achieve this turning task, I generally use a ½″ roundnose, a ¾″ square nose scraper, and a ½″ square chisel. While the first two tools are used for removing wood, I use the chisel for making the lid (when required) and glass insert shoulders. The chisel, used as a scraper, is also excellent for cleaning and squaring the bottom of the box where the movement is to be placed.

Another tool I use in turning music boxes is a standard ½″ skewed chisel. I use it to make slight indentations in the center of the bottom of the box where a hole will be drilled for chuck mounting. I also find this tool helpful in turning the base of a musical box when it is mounted on a chuck. The base area is necessary for the free movement of the musical mechanism's winding key and I have found the chisel's skew to be very effective in creating this area. One of the reasons I use chisels in this manner is that they allow me to make very light and specific cuts with good tool control.

I always sharpen my square noses, skewed scrapers, and, when used, gouges on an electric grinder mounted with a 1″-carborundum medium wheel. While the grinder has a metal tool guide, my grinding is somewhat of a freehand technique. I always wear a full face mask when using the grinder. My roundnose scrapers, and others that I use, along with the smaller chisels, are almost always sharpened on a 6″ × 48″ belt sander. Usually the sander is set up with either a 100- or 120-grit belt. The tools are sharpened on about a 2″ strip of the belt near one edge. This prevents ruining the entire belt, which, obviously, is used for other purposes. I have found this method of sharpening reasonably fast, simple, and effective for my purposes. Refer to the additional resources listed in the bibliography for this chapter; there is a considerable body of literature that deals with the specific use and sharpening of turning tools. Also, I would strongly urge you to rely on your own problem-solving skills to develop turning tech-

the piece. On smaller boxes, lids, and bowls, I usually begin with a ½″ roundnose again, pointed down. The scraper is pointed downwards to assure that the upper edge is in contact with the wood. I also use roundnoses for roughing the inside of pieces and, depending upon the design, often for finishing. Most of my tools are what are generally referred to as being "long and strong." In addition to the longer handle, this type of tool has a thicker and longer tine, more steel, to reduce vibration or chatter. They are also substantially easier to control when turning.

If the shape permits, I often finish turning the outside of pieces with extra-heavy skewed scrapers (Illus. 2-7). These scrapers are ⅜″ thick and 1½″ wide and very effective in faceplate turning. They, and other designs, are also available without handles.

niques that are useful and productive for you. Trying to duplicate the techniques recommended by others can often result in a great many frustrating and futile experiences.

Abrasive Paper Finishing

When the musical box, or whatever it is that I've been turning, is shaped and tool-finished, I use a series of abrasive papers to complete the project. As stated earlier, when finishing I run the lathe at 2220 rpm. In addition to wearing gloves, I use pieces of foam carpeting pad as sanding blocks. This material is thick, yet flexible enough to allow the finishing of all surfaces regardless of design. Also, the pad absorbs the friction heat from the paper that would otherwise burn the wood. I usually quarter a full sheet of abrasive paper and then fold the quarter sections, using one surface and then the other. On most of the hardwoods, and at lathe finishing speeds, most abrasive papers break down rather quickly. Thus I tend to use a lot of paper when finishing.

According to the type of wood and the quality of the surface achieved with the turning tools, I decide what grit abrasive paper to use at the start.

Another significant variable in choice of grit is the quality of finish on the cross-grain section of the piece. With a number of the hardwoods, scraping as a turning method does not effectively deal with the cross grains of the wood. In those instances where the scrapers have not been effective with the cross grain, I use abrasive papers and reverse the rotation of the block.

I have mounted a drum switch on my lathe that permits, when needed, the reversal of the motor and thus the reversal of the spindle and the faceplate assembly. When the cross grains will not clear up in the forward mode, I reverse the spindle and attack the grain from the opposite direction. In time, this process usually will solve the problem. One caution with this reversing capability. If the faceplate is not tight on the spindle, the initial reverse thrust can loosen the assembly and throw it off the lathe.

In most instances, I begin finishing with 100-grit garnet paper, open face, using a minimum of pressure. With this grit, my primary target is usually the cross-grain section of the piece. If necessary, I will move from the forward to the reverse mode a number of times. This process deals with the desire of the grain to lay down and look

Illus. 2-8 Lid Designs for Music Boxes

"mousey." If the 100-grit will not clear up the cross grain, I will, if necessary, use a 60-grit. In using such coarse grit, if too much pressure is applied on the pad and paper, severe scratching will occur on the wood surface. Use these coarse grits sparingly and with great care. Next, I use 150-grit followed by either a 220- or 240-grit, again in garnet paper. Using the sanding pad, I begin applying a bit more pressure as I move into the finer grits. I first target and remove any scratches that the previous grit may have made in the wood. Then, the finishing process focuses on the entire piece, both inside and out. With music boxes and bowls, I seldom use abrasive paper in that section where the musical movement is placed. It is not significantly visible once the movement has been placed on the base. Also, abrasive papers tend to grind off the sharp edges of the insert and lid shoulders in the pieces.

Next in finishing I use either 280- or 320-grit silicon carbide wet or dry paper. Normally I will use this cloth-type paper dry but, on occasion, I will moisten it. On some of the pieces I will also use 600-grit wet or dry. All pieces receive a final going over with 4/0 steel wool.

With the spalted woods, I always add one additional step to the front end of the process. I use 60-grit on heavy paper before moving to the finer grits. As you may know, the spalted woods require a great deal of finishing work in addition to quantities of abrasive paper. It is mandatory on the spalted woods that you get to the harder portions of the block.

Preparing Special Blocks and Lids

Preliminaries

In addition to the wide range of woods available in form ready to use for turning music boxes and other pieces, there are a number of techniques for preparing special blocks. While most woods can clearly stand on their own and need little, if any, embellishment, a few of them need help. I have found too, that by using a few special techniques I can salvage some pieces in addition to maximizing scraps. The range of possibilities in designing and preparing special turning blocks is only limited by your ingenuity, the woods available, and, to a lesser degree, your skill with tools.

My interest in using veneers and other special type of wood in turning has emerged from practical necessity. Frequently, some of the air dried and, on occasion, the kiln dried larger stock will develop splits or checks. The size and nature of the splits all too often preclude using the material for larger turnings. Rather than cutting the stock into smaller pieces in order to salvage at least a portion of the wood, I will laminate the larger pieces at the point of the split. Usually I will use veneer, but solid woods will also work.

The same desire to maximize materials, along with enhancement of the pieces, carries over to designing and preparing lids for musical boxes. Lids for boxes can be designed and turned using veneers and solid scraps. Scraps also lend themselves to use as decorative plugs in both boxes and lids. With a few tools and some rather simple procedures, the opportunities for creative designs are endless. While our discussions will focus on special blocks and lids for music boxes and bowls, the procedures can be applied to faceplate-turning blocks for any purpose.

Lids and Their Preparation

While Illus. 2-8 pictures some of the standard lid designs that I use with musical boxes, they are only a sampling of the possibilities. Part of the pleasure in turning is to sketch possible designs on paper. In addition to sketching, I stack different types of wood to see how they relate to one

Illus. 2-9 Lids from Solid Blocks: Rough and Finished

another. It's important to plan your project but it's fun to design it as well.

Lids for boxes can be made and turned from one solid piece of wood (Illus. 2-9). The wood that is used for the lid can be the same as used in the box or something entirely different. While I have found that some of the woods tend to clash with one another, your experience and preference may be different. I often save pieces of quartered red or white oak to use as lids from solids; in walnut, I watch for pieces that have a satin figure in them. As the lid is the most conspicuous portion of the box, when using solids I try to be very selective with the woods to be used.

Another variable to consider with solid lids is their thickness and eventual turned height in relation to the box. I seek to use materials that have not been surfaced, thus allowing more wood to work with when turning. I have found that an additional one-eighth inch of thickness can be critical in both lid and box turning.

For lids that are to be placed on an inside shoulder in a box, I pattern them from one-fourth inch to three-eighths inch larger than the diameter of the finished box. This allows sufficient wood for turning the lid down to size. I use a template or compass to pattern the lid circles and then cut them with a band saw. As I discuss under chucks, and in later chapters, I mark the midpoint of the lids as they are being traced. This center point is where a hole will be drilled for mounting the lid on a chuck for turning.

In addition to the solid lid, another design is to glue a small round block on the lid base for turning as a decorative but functional knob. Illus. 2-10 pictures this layout, along with some finished lids. The eventual height of the turned lid and knob must be in proper relation to the box: not too tall, not too short. Frequently I use small blocks at least 1½″ (6/4's) thick to glue on the lid blocks for knobs. This allows sufficient wood for turning knobs that are the right height for most boxes.

Knobs are another item that require prior pencil-and-paper design work. I tend, often from habit, to turn knobs of the same basic appearance, an approach that limits one in the possibilities for different designs. As you will discover, the base of the lid can be turned in many different designs that in part will dictate or suggest a knob design. On occasion I use different woods for the lid base and knob, which provides an excellent effect for a lid.

Illus. 2-10 Lids with Knobs: Rough and Finished

As suggested, the lids should be cut at least ¼″ larger than the diameter of the finished box. This type of lid fits into a recessed shoulder in the box. The smaller block that will become the knob should be at least 1¼″ in diameter and, as indicated, approximately 1½″ high. With the exception of a large music box, these dimensions are adequate for most lids.

To assure good gluing surfaces, after cutting the lid and knob block round, sand them, with the grain, on a belt sander. Using a yellow glue on both surfaces, place the knob block in the center of the lid block and clamp. Be certain, when clamping, that the knob block doesn't slide off-center of the lid block. Once aligned and clamped, allow the assembly to dry (Illus. 2-11).

Illus. 2-11 Preparing a Lid with Knob

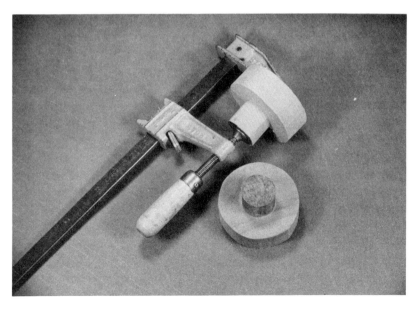

Another lid design is to laminate a different solid wood to either the lid block or knob block; Illus. 2-12 shows examples of this design both before and after turning. It can give an interesting effect to the lid. To simplify the gluing and clamping process for this design, work with the blocks squared. This approach also allows for the use of scraps. However, if scraps to be used are not of the same thickness as the lid or knob blocks, be certain that they are flush with the bases of both. This will simplify gluing and turning.

In cutting pieces to glue either on the lid or knob block, you have a wide range of options. The simplest design is to cut the lid or knob block and the pieces in straight lines. You can, however, cut them at almost any angle you desire and that your equipment will allow. Prior to gluing and clamping the various pieces together, lightly sand the cut surfaces. When the gluing and clamping process is completed, trace the lid and knob round for cutting.

Plugs from different woods can also be used in lids as a design option. If precision of plug placement is desired, after mounting the block on the lathe use the indexing mechanism. My personal preference in plugging is to be less exacting in my designs and how I want the end product to look. In general I use only one or two plugs in a lid design. Illus. 2-13 shows both the layouts and the finished lids. On occasion I will use a third plug to overlap the other two plugs. I have also found that matching and, on occasion, contrasting woods used for plugs can be an important design consideration. A few well-placed plugs of appropriate woods tend to enhance the lid rather than overwhelm it.

I use either a three-eighths inch or one-half inch plug cutter mounted on the drill press for cutting plugs. They are cut to the same thickness as the lid block. This is done so that the plugs show on the bottom of the lid as well as on the top, making for a curious double effect. The plugs are always cut from scraps.

Holes for the plugs are drilled in the lid using the appropriate diameter spur or Forstner bit. In drilling holes, be certain that they are placed far enough in from the edge of the lid. Placement of the holes, by design, tends to cluster in one area of the lid: I seek to avoid balance in their placement. In gluing, I place yellow glue on both the walls of the holes and on the plugs. If you want the grain of the plug and lid to match, place the plug accordingly. Lightly tap the plugs into the holes being careful not to split the lid.

If the plug-overlap design is wanted, drill only one hole in the lid, insert the plug, and allow to dry. For the second plug that is to partially overlap the first, drill the second hole in the lid through that portion of the first plug that you want to overlap. Place the second glued plug and allow to dry. This process, if desired, can be repeated until you have a cluster of overlapping plugs of either the same or different woods. Be certain you allow the plugs to dry adequately between each step. An alternative design is to use plugs of different diameters in the cluster.

Veneers can also be used in making lids or knobs for music and other boxes (Illus. 2-14). To facilitate the gluing and clamping process, when using veneer on lids, I work with square blocks. As veneers are available in one-thirty-second inch thickness, the design possibilities with this fragile but flexible material are challenging. For both lids and bowls I use the least expensive veneer I can obtain: since only the edges are visible in the turned piece, there is no need for high-quality figured veneer. Most of my veneering on turning blocks is done using either ash or walnut. These two woods, a light and a dark, provide sufficient contrast for most of the blocks I want to laminate.

I trace the lid or knob circle in a block but do not cut it out. This is followed by determining where on the lid or knob the veneer strip is to run; should it run straight or at an angle? Also, would two or more intersecting veneer strips be appropriate? In essence, try to visualize, and thus design, how the lid or knob will look when finished. While the design can be cut freehand on the band saw, I usually pencil the desired cut on the surface of the lid or knob. After cutting the block in two pieces, I lightly sand the surfaces, being careful not to cut

Illus. 2-12 Laminated Lids: Rough and Finished

Illus. 2-13 Lids with Plugs: Rough and Finished

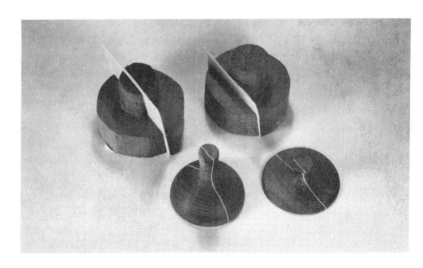

Ilus. 2-14 Lids with Veneer: Rough and Finished

off the edges. With a pair of scissors, I cut the veneer to the width and length desired.

Match the grain direction of the veneer and the block. It's a good idea to cut the veneer wider and longer than required unless your measurements are precise. After cleaning all surfaces, apply yellow glue to both faces of the block and the veneer; be certain the glue is spread on the entire surface. Then place the veneer strip between the two pieces of the block and clamp. When clamping, align your lid on the circle pattern lines and be sure to have good and equal pressure on all sides. Allow to dry and then cut as marked.

These are only a few ideas for preparing lids for music or other boxes. As you will discover, not only the lids but especially the knobs present the turner with opportunities for creative turning. Many other designs are discussed in the various references at the end of this chapter.

Specific methods for turning lids are discussed in later chapters detailing how to make specific types of music boxes. As you will discover, I turn my box lids using chucks and the tailstock.

Boxes with Tray and Lid

While most music boxes lend themselves, by design, to some capacity for storing items, the music box with a tray offers even greater functionality. In general, I use two basic tray/box designs; in that both require some preparations prior to turning, I consider them to be special blocks.

In most instances I use the same type of wood for the lid, box, and tray, but you can use different woods for each part if desired. Also, for my purposes, I have standardized both the dimensions and the basic designs of the boxes with trays. Thus, those specific details that follow relate to my preferences. As always, explore your own design and dimensional ideas for such types of special turning blocks.

For the larger box/tray design, I prepare a 9″-diameter round block. Using a school compass, I draw the circle upon rough stock generally anywhere from 1″ (4/4's) to 1½″ (6/4's) thick. Thinner

stock is clearly acceptable, but it does limit the eventual height of the edge of the tray. I seek to have a raised tray edge so that it can function as a serving unit if desired. Previously I have examined the wood to determine which side should be the top surface of the tray before, using the compass, I trace the 9″-diameter circle on the top surface. In using the compass, make a deep penetration with the point at the center of the circle. This tracing is followed in cutting the circle on the band saw.

After the tray has been cut round, I sand the top surface smooth to provide an effective gluing surface for the box that will be attached. Using the midpoint hole in the tray, I trace, lightly, a 3½″-diameter circle on the top surface of the tray, which circle will serve as a guide when gluing the round 3½″-diameter block on the tray surface. This simplifies the centering process and thus the eventual turning of the assembly.

The next procedure is to prepare the round block that will be glued to the tray and will, eventually, hold the music movement and lid. I use stock that is at least 2″ (8/4's) thick. That thickness, along with a lid with a knob, is visually in proportion to the 9″ tray. Also, that thickness allows ample space for housing the music movement, as well as some storage area inside the box. Using either a template or compass, I pattern and cut the 3½″-diameter circle block. If the desired base end is rough, I belt-sand it to a surface ready for gluing.

After spreading yellow glue on both the marked area on the tray and on the base of the box, the movement block is placed inside the tray-circle area and clamped. In clamping, be careful that the block does not slide off-center when tightening the clamp. Allow sufficient drying time before turning (Illus. 2-15).

The type of lid desired for this design can be determined and prepared in accordance with the methods discussed in the previous section. To maintain a sense of proportion, I use the lid-with-knob design with the larger box/tray unit.

The second box/tray design is essentially the

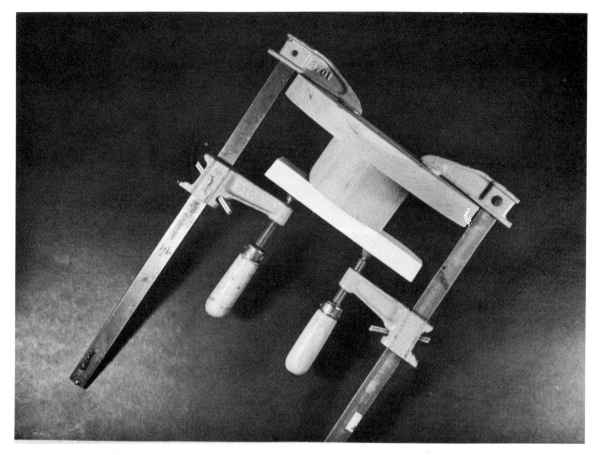

Illus. 2-15 Large Music Box and Tray: Glued and Clamped Blocks

same as the first, only smaller. The base piece, when turned, provides more of a trench area than a tray. While the first design lends itself to use as a decorative or functional serving tray, the smaller unit is better used for jewelry or some dresser-top purpose.

The small unit is also a glued assembly, but it is designed with a 5½"-diameter base. The box portion of the unit is 3½" in diameter, the same as for the larger box/tray. Preparation and gluing procedures are also the same for this assembly.

If desired, both of these box/tray designs lend themselves to the use of veneer or plugs. Use the techniques described earlier. It is best, however, to complete the veneering process before cutting either the tray or box blocks round. As you may

recall, this simplifies and makes for more effective clamping of the glued pieces.

Laminating Blocks

While the use of veneer in turning blocks can help some of the less exciting woods—on the whole I prefer turning solid blocks without benefit of embellishment. This preference applies especially to the larger turning blocks that I use for musical bowls. When I have, for example, walnut stock that runs from 4" (16/4's) to 6" (24/4's), I find it a travesty to cut them and use veneer or anything else. However, because much of my larger turning stock is graded #3 and is often air dried, it does develop some radial checks and splits that prevent using it for solid blocks. These defects often necessitate cutting and veneering to salvage 'the wood. Illus. 2-16 shows finished music bowls that were veneered because of splits or checks in the blocks.

If the check is minor, I may turn the block, leaving the walls thick in the area of the check. With some blocks, just before finishing on the lathe, I will force white glue into the check and clamp it with a belt clamp. This method is usually effective, but the excess glue on the surface must be removed or it will stain the wood.

Illus. 2-17 shows blocks that have been laminated with veneer along splits or bad checks. After the excess veneer is trimmed, these blocks will be ready for turning. Unless there is more than one serious defect in the block, I will only cut the block once and use a single strip of veneer. Too much veneer tends to cheapen the appearance of the piece. This preference is compromised on occasion when I find two or more serious checks in a block. Illus. 2-18 presents some veneered blocks that required multiple strips because of numerous defects.

In cutting turning blocks to insert veneer, the band saw is the tool of choice. After locating the defect I want to cut through, I pencil in a cutting line. With large blocks, I try to avoid cutting them in straight lines. Frequently it is necessary to adjust the band saw table to accommodate an angle cut dictated by the check or split. Once the saw is aligned, I cut through the check, following the premarked line (Illus. 2-19). The placement of the veneer at a curve gives an interesting effect in the finished piece. As reported earlier, my band saw is normally set up with a ¼" skip blade with 5½ teeth per inch. This blade allows for cutting curves but it also gives a fairly clean cutting surface.

After cutting the block, I may do some hand sanding on the two surfaces. The amount of sanding is largely determined by the quality of the band saw cut. Unless a coarse band saw blade is used, a minimum of sanding is usually required.

Illus. 2-16 Large Bowls with Veneer: Finished

*Illus. 2-17 Large Bowl
Blocks with Veneer: Rough*

*Illus. 2-18 Finished Bowls
with Multiple Veneer Strips*

*Illus. 2-19 Cutting a Bowl
Block to Insert Veneer*

Minor roughness on the edges does not show after the veneer is glued in place.

These preparations of the block are followed by cutting a piece of appropriately colored veneer that is somewhat longer and wider than required. If desired, you can stack any number of veneer pieces to laminate between the two pieces of block; I tend to use only one strip of veneer.

Spread yellow glue on both surfaces of the veneer and also the blocks. Be certain that there is glue over the entire surface. Place the veneer against the face of one piece of block, followed by placement of the second (Illus. 2-20). I keep the veneer flush at its bottom edge with both block bases. This tends to simplify assembling and clamping the glued pieces. The veneer usually overlaps at the top and on both sides of the blocks. I use bar clamps, strategically placed, to clamp the entire assembly together (Illus. 2-21). As you will discover, the clamping process can be difficult since the blocks and veneer are inclined to slide out of position because of the glue. Some imagination and varying placement of the clamps eventually will solve the problem. Clamping round blocks is always difficult so, when possible, I do my veneering when the block is square.

The veneering process is also applicable to smaller blocks, which can be used with the box/tray design or as standard music boxes with lids. Square blocks that are also a standard music box design can also be veneered, if desired. The square blocks lend themselves to compound cuts and other different possibilities with veneer. The end product can be quite exciting.

Turning blocks can also be laminated with other solid strips or blocks of wood. There is no end of treatments in preparing special turning blocks. It's a superb way to maximize your scraps and be creative at the same time.

Decorative Plugs

The use of plugs was discussed under preparation of box lids and the same process can be used with bowl or box blocks. A single plug or a cluster of plugs can give a piece an interesting appearance. My preference is to use plugs sparingly. In Illus. 2-22 you see blocks that have been plugged and are ready for turning. Plugs cut from padouk or bubinga, because of their reddish color, look nice in a bowl or box. Hedge, because of its unusual

Illus. 2-21 Veneered Block Glued and Clamped

yellowish color, and bocote, because it is so different, both make excellent plug woods. Any woods that contrast either in color or grain seem to be effective plug material.

After planning the design and placement of the plugs on the block, I drill the appropriate premarked holes using a drill press, and, as recommended earlier, a sharp spur or Forstner bit of matching diameter to the plug size. I drill the holes in the round block that has been cut to its

Illus. 2-22 Turning Blocks with Plugs

turning diameter. Usually the roundness of the block presents no problem when drilling the plug holes. However, to avoid movement when drilling, clamp the block to the drill press table.

Before tapping the plugs into the drilled holes, spread yellow glue along the walls of the holes and also some on the plugs. Splitting is seldom a problem with solid blocks but care should be taken in driving the plugs into the holes. If you want the grain of the plugs and the block to match, this is the time for that alignment process. After the plugs have dried, using a hacksaw, saw them reasonably flush with the wall of the block. If the plugs are protruding too far while the block is being turned, they can be ripped out, shattered, or splintered.

For cluster designs with plugs, refer to the earlier discussion under preparation of lids. The procedures are the same for a box or bowl.

Other Possibilities

Needless to say, there are any number of ways to prepare specialized blocks for turning boxes and bowls. For those inclined to laminate solids to build their own turning blocks, a number of excellent references are provided. There are also references to woodturners who are exploring nontraditional shapes in turned objects. It is hoped, however, that other possibilities for preparing turning blocks will proceed from your own creativity. I'm not certain what they may be, but I'm confident they're out there waiting to be discovered by some innovative woodturner.

Faceplate Chucks and Screw Centers

Preliminaries

The use of faceplate chucks is mandatory to a number of procedures in turning musical boxes or bowls. By definition, a chuck is a device that holds something. In this case it is a hardwood device with a screw in its end, mounted on a faceplate that allows for the turning of music boxes, lids, and bowls. While there are any number of commercial chucks available, I try to design and craft my own based on specific needs. It's a great deal of fun and it's also substantially cheaper to make your own. One minor problem with my method is that it does tie up a number of faceplates if you make more than one chuck. You can, however, remove and replace them on the faceplate if desired.

Before discussing in detail the making of chucks, a few additional comments abut faceplate turning are in order. In turning the larger blocks and also when using a chuck, it is common for the faceplate to lock tight on the mandrel or spindle of the headstock. As a result of heat buildup and cooling, plus the force of turning, faceplates often

Illus. 2-23 "O" Rings for Lathe Headstock Spindle

Illus. 2-24 Self-made Chucks: Long and Short Designs

become almost impossible to remove from the mandrel. To eliminate this problem, I use what plumbers call "O" rings (Illus. 2-23). Basically an "O" ring is a round rubber ring manufactured in various diameters. I buy the diameter ring that will fit over the mandrel of my lathe and slide it against the metal base. Cork or fibre rings are also effective if you can find or make them. While the "O" rings do not eliminate the problem totally, they do cut down on its frequency. Two wrenches are always available as a backup system.

With regard to chucks, I have found that the first design presented meets most needs in turning music boxes and lids. It is, however, limited in terms of use for larger musical bowls. The first design, because it is shorter, has more stability and is less inclined to rotate a piece off-center while turning. With both designs I use the tailstock as a support and safety system when turning. In general, I will operate the lathe at 2220 rpm when using chucks, with a notable exception when using a chuck for turning a bowl off-center. In this instance I reduce the speed to 990 rpm. More about these details later.

Chuck Design 1

Illus. 2-24 shows both finished chuck designs; they are essentially the same except for their lengths. Primarily because of its availability, I usually use red or white oak for making chucks. Design 1 requires stock that is at least 2″ (8/4's) thick. In addition to a 3″ or comparable size faceplate, the chuck requires lag screws that are ¼″ × 3″. A standard socket set, a small triangle or round file, and a ⅛″ high-speed drill bit are also necessary. A Dremel tool with a metal cutting stone is a good alternative to a file.

Using a template or pencil compass, trace a 3½″-diameter circle on the stock to be used. You can first trace, then cut and turn either vertically to or horizontally with the grain. Both seem equally effective. Cut the block on the band saw, and mount the faceplate using at least ½″ wood screws. Mount the assembly on the lathe, bringing forward the tailstock for support. After turning the entire block round, tool a shaft that is at least 1⅝″ long and 2½″ in diameter. Use a preset vernier caliper, if available, to determine the proper diameter. While you are turning the shaft from the front to the back of the block, watch for your faceplate screws. You clearly do not want them to be hit with a tool if it can be helped; it dulls the tool and ruins the screws.

Remove the tailstock and align the tool rest for cleaning off the outer face of the chuck. After turning it flat, make a small indentation in the center of the face, using a skew or similar chisel.

This hole will mark the center point for drilling through the entire chuck for placement of the lag screw. Remove the assembly from the lathe.

The next step depends on the type of faceplate you use. Some faceplates are hollow from the threaded area through the plate surface. For this type of plate, drill a ⅛″ hole, starting at the small indentation on the face of the chuck, through the entire unit. A drill press is recommended. Do not remove the faceplate during this procedure with this type of faceplate unit. It is important that the hole be drilled perfectly straight, otherwise the lag screw will be too far off-center. With the faceplate still attached to the chuck, using a socket set, screw the lag from the back of the chuck all the way through. The lag screw threads should protrude approximately 1″ from the face of the chuck.

If your faceplate has a metal facing at the end of the threaded shaft, you may need to proceed differently in placing the lag screw. Some faceplates have a screw hole in this section of the faceplate. If it is large enough to accommodate the ¼″-diameter lag screw, drill a ⅛″ hole, beginning at the indentation on the face, through the entire assembly. Using a socket set, screw in the lag.

Some faceplates will not permit either of the two methods for placement of the lag screw. In these instances the faceplate must be removed from the chuck. Before removal, however, clearly make alignment lines on the edge of the faceplate and the chuck. When reassembling, this allows the unit to remain centered. Drill a ⅛″ hole as described. You will also have to drill out an area on the back of the chuck to accommodate the head of the lag screw. Using a socket, screw in the lag and reassemble the chuck and the faceplate.

Before mounting the chuck back on the lathe, use a grinder to grind off the tapered point of the lag screw. In order that the threads of the lag will grip the wood more effectively, you need to grind or file between the threads. I use a Dremel tool with a small stone to deepen the gullets of the lag screw. If the Dremel is used, wear a mask. A triangle or round file, if small enough, will also work. As suggested, this deepening of the area

between the threads greatly increases the holding power of the screw when a turning block is screwed on the chuck.

The next step is to place the unit on the lathe and test it. If the chuck is a bit off-center, true it up with a turning tool. On occasion the lag screw seems off-center. If you watch it while rotating, you can usually determine which side it seems to be rotating towards. While the unit is rotating, tap the screw lightly with a block of wood in the opposite direction. A number of taps are generally required before it will run reasonably true.

I find, after using chucks for a while, that I need to retighten the faceplate screws. Also, I reshape the chuck walls with a turning tool when it begins to run off-center. In general, this type of chuck will give excellent service for many turnings, although, in time, it will have to be discarded and another made. The different ways that I use this chuck are demonstrated in the chapters that discuss turning music boxes.

Chuck Design 2

This chuck is essentially the same basic design as the preceding one, but it is longer and requires a few additional procedures to make. I use the second chuck primarily for large bowls that will have music movements set in them. Because of its length, on occasion it presents some off-center problems. It needs a bit more attention in maintaining it than does its shorter counterpart, but it is a very effective device for turning out the bottoms of bowls to be used as music boxes.

Oak is usually the wood of choice for this chuck. I try to find 4″ × 4″ cut-offs or stacking material that is sufficiently dry to use for this design. The chuck needs to be at least 3½″ long. I have found such length adequate to accommodate most of the larger bowls I turn. Using a template or compass, trace a 3½″ circle on the stock. In relation to the grain, lay out this chuck vertically rather than horizontally. Before cutting the block round, trim it back to a full 3½″ length. After cutting, mount the block on the faceplate.

I generally turn this chuck to a 2½″ diameter on the forward section of the block, approximately 1¼″ in length. You can use a vernier caliper to check the dimensions. The balance of the chuck is tapered to an outer limit of 3″. I use the tapered section of the chuck to prepare wooden rings for use as decorative coverings over the glass inserts in music boxes. (More about this later.) After the chuck wall has been turned, finish the face surface as described under Chuck 1. Remember to make a small indentation or hole in the surface of the chuck face.

As with the other chuck design, the next steps in the process are determined by the type of faceplate being used. However, because of the increased length of this chuck, the ⅛″ drill hole needs to be only 2″ deep. The next procedure is also different. For the lag screw to protrude the minimum of 1″ from the face of the chuck, a hole large enough to accommodate the head of the lag screw must be drilled in the base. To accommodate both the head of the lag screw and a socket

for screwing it into the chuck, use a ¾″-diameter wood bit. Assuming your chuck is 3½″ long, the drilled ¾″-diameter hole should be at least 1½″ deep. With a 3″ lag screw, this allows for a 1″ threaded projection from the face of the chuck. If it is necessary to remove the chuck from the faceplate for drilling, be certain to make alignment markings on the edges of the plate and the chuck for reassembly.

Following the placement of the lag screw through the chuck, grind off the tapered point of the screw. As indicated earlier, the lag screw shaft should be a uniform diameter for maximum holding capacity. Also, the gullets of the screw should again be deepened using the methods previously described. If a Dremel is used, remember to wear eye or face protection.

Mount the finished assembly on the lathe. If the chuck, when rotating, is off-center, lightly turn it back to shape. The lag screw, if off-center, can be tapped for alignment. The specific uses for this chuck are discussed in detail in later chapters.

Screw-Center Design

While the screw-center is not mandatory for turning music boxes, it does, on occasion, provide a definite service. Illus. 2-25 is of one of my screw-centers; I sometimes use a screw-center with a shim to turn box lids. The shim separates the item being turned from the screw-center face, thus preventing the ruining of the center's surface. As you will discover, the screw-center offers more stability for turning some pieces than do chucks.

The screw-center unit can be made from most hardwood stock. It should, however, be at least 1″ (4/4's) thick, which thickness allows for ample penetration by the faceplate screws. For this unit, use a 2″ × 12 pan head tapping screw, a screw that, unlike the lag screw, is threaded along the entire length of the shaft. Thus it is able to grip the screw-center wood disc totally as it penetrates; this reduces and, frequently, totally eliminates slippage of the screw in the center disc. The pan-head does not lend itself to use in chucks because

Illus. 2-25 Self-made Screw-center

of its slotted head. The slot is usually stripped by a standard screwdriver before it can penetrate the entire length of the longer chucks.

To make the screw-center unit, pattern a disc that is 3½″ in diameter from 1″ (4/4's) stock. After cutting the disc, mount it on a 3″ faceplate with appropriate screws. Turn the edge on the lathe so that it is a round, balanced disc. Using a skew or similar tool, cut an indentation at the center point on the front surface of the disc. As with the chucks, this is the point of penetration for the panhead screw.

Depending on the type of faceplate used, ⅛″ hole is drilled through the disc using the surface indentation as the guide. If the faceplate must be removed, make alignment marks on the plate and disc edges for reassembly. Also, with some plates, you may have to drill a small hole in the back surface of the disc to accommodate the screw-head.

After the screw has been placed in the center of the unit, use a hack saw to cut off any length in excess of ¾″, the screw should extend ¾″ from the front surface. Deepen the gullets of the screw as described under the chuck procedures, providing a greater holding capacity for the blocks that are screwed to the unit for turning. Incidentally, when using the screw-center in turning, also use the tailstock for support and safety.

Finishing: The Total Process

Preliminaries

One of the advantages of working with most of the hardwoods is that, when turned, they lend themselves to natural-look finishes. No stains are necessary. I never use stains on any of my turned pieces, whether crafted from the hardwoods or pine. My goal in finishing is to allow the wood to be as natural as possible. Finishes can be used either to enhance the natural appearance of the wood or to distract from it. With few exceptions, woods do require some type of finish; the issue is very simply a matter of with what kind of material and how it is to be done. While the use of stains is a matter of personal preference, I encourage you at least to try the natural-look finishes that are available.

The function of the piece is a factor to consider in its finishing; items that are handled a great deal do not necessarily need a heavy surface-type finish, i.e., one that is built up. The surface of most woods is rather tolerant of handling and, in many instances, will become more attractive as a result of it. On the other hand, if the piece is to be used to hold food items, care must be taken to use only nontoxic finishing products, regardless of the type of finish desired.

There are two basic types of finishes: penetrating and nonpenetrating. The penetrating finishes are the various oils that are available; they are literally absorbed into the wood surface. The oils penetrate, preserve, protect, and greatly enhance the appearance of the wood without leaving a covering or coating on the surface. The other type of finish, the nonpenetrating, usually leaves some form of coating on the surface of the wood. The finish is a series of built-up surface coats of some product, usually a shellac, lacquer, polyurethane, varnish or one of various types of wax. New technologies have resulted in a proliferation of different types of finishing products that are available. To assist you in targeting a few, I will identify and discuss specific products that I use in my shop for both penetrating and nonpenetrating finishes. I will also discuss how both basic approaches can be combined to provide a very attractive and durable finished product. While the methods and products discussed can be used for any kind of turned piece, the focus will be on finishing musical boxes and bowls.

Finishes of both major types can be used on turned pieces that are either on or off the faceplate and lathe. There are advantages and disadvantages to both approaches, as well as the distinct difference in the end products. With music boxes, by the nature of how they are turned, at no point are they completely ready for a total on-lathe finishing process. You can finish the most conspicuous sections of a music box, lid, and bowl while on the lathe. Other less noticeable portions, for example, the base, the inside, and the bottom of the lid, must then be finished off-lathe. My preference is for off-lathe finishings and, with music boxes and bowls, it is often much easier. It is definitely worth trying both methods and then making a decision based on your own experience and preferences.

Ideally, both types of finishes should be applied in a clean, dust-free atmosphere. While the penetrating finishes do not require the ideal, it is still desirable. Reality, at least in my own shop, is always far removed from the ideal. The setting for finishing, as detailed on product labels, was written, I suspect, by nonwoodworkers. In that my shop does not lend itself to the finishing environment usually recommended, I have learned to compromise the finishing process. For example I rarely use varnish or polyurethane simply because they take too long to dry. Decisions about the finishing process and the products to use must take into account such considerations.

The following discussion assumes that the item to be finished has been adequately prepared with abrasive papers and steel wool. While a number of these abrasives can and will be used in some finishing techniques, proper earlier preparation of the surface is assumed. The use of abrasive papers was described earlier in this chapter.

On-Lathe Finishes

On-lathe finishes are achieved while the piece is mounted on the lathe in either a fixed or rotating position. This method permits the achievement of extremely hard, highly polished finishes that are preferred by many turners. Also, some suggest that the on-lathe method makes possible a more uniform and lasting surface finish. A limiting factor in this method, especially when finishing musical boxes or bowls, is the inability to finish the entire project at one time. Another limiting factor is that it can tie up faceplates, chucks, and, on occasion, the lathe itself. It frequently also necessitates finishing a single piece immediately after it has been turned. I prefer finishing a number of pieces at the same time in order to minimize the mess and maximize my time. Again, none of these limitations is especially significant, particularly to the hobbyist turner. It is an area of personal preference and how you tend to operate in your own shop.

One on-lathe finish for music boxes and other pieces can be achieved with shellac, a nonpenetrating surface product. In using shellac for finishing, you can obtain a glossy, hard, high-quality finish and, if desired, a French-polish-type finish. The French polish method involves more work and the use of boiled linseed oil with the shellac.

I purchase prepared white shellac that generally comes designated as 3-pound cut. This pound-cut designation refers to the weight of shellac that is dissolved in a gallon of solvent alcohol. For example, the 3-pound cut that I purchase literally means that the formula used was a ratio of three pounds of shellac to one gallon of alcohol. When buying shellac, you should also obtain a quantity of denatured alcohol for cutting it further as needed. If preferred, shellac flakes can be purchased in bulk from some suppliers and the user can prepare it with alcohol as needed. A word of caution. Prepared shellac is usually, or should be, dated because it has a limited shelf life. Old shellac tends to lose both its durability and also its quick-drying capacity.

Some finishers prefer orange shellac to white when working with the darker hardwoods. I have found that the orange does look better on walnut, but this is an area of personal preference. Both types are generally used the same way.

In using shellac as an on-lathe finish, I mix a pint of 3-pound cut with a pint of solvent alcohol as the initial step in the process. However, a word of warning before the next step. After applying the shellac and turning on the lathe, the rotation of the piece throws off the wet shellac. It's a good idea to stand aside for a moment and also to wear eye protection. You may want to remove any wood or other items that could be spattered with shellac when the lathe is turned on.

Before applying the shellac-alcohol mixture to the piece as it's mounted on the lathe, have a number of large lint-free rags at hand. After the shellac has been applied, using brush or rag, turn on the lathe and allow the piece to rotate for a few seconds. This allows the shellac to begin drying. As you might surmise, the high concentration of alcohol in the mixture speeds up the drying process even more. While the piece is still rotating, stretch a rag firmly between both hands and apply it to the surface of the piece. Move the rag back and forth along the surface. Fold and apply the rag to the inside, under pressure, if it too is being finished. The speed of the lathe plus the rag with pressure creats heat via friction that quickly dries the surface. The rag also evens out the shellac on the surface. For this process, I run my lathe at 2220 rpm.

The first shellac-alcohol application functions as a sealer. It also tends to raise fine hairs on the surface of the wood, especially in areas of cross grain. With the lathe running, lightly go over the entire surface with a 320-grit or finer abrasive paper. Carefully clean the piece with a rag or tack cloth, then apply another coat of the mixture and repeat the entire process. Following the second and subsequent applications, rub the dry surface lightly with 4/0 steel wool rather than abrasive paper. Be certain to clean the steel hairs off the surface between applications.

As the surface covering begins to develop as a result of the shellac-alcohol mixture, change to applying the undiluted 3-pound shellac. Depending on both temperature and humidity, this shellac cut requires more drying time on the lathe and also between coats. Even though the rag is used in the same fashion, the friction-generated heat does not adequately dry the shellac. Too much pressure with the rag can, at this stage of finishing, burn the shellac surface. Allowing for drying periods between coats, add as many additional applications of shellac as desired. Be certain to use, very lightly, 4/0 steel wool between coats, and clean the surface.

When you have achieved a finish that satisfies, rub the piece one final time with 4/0 steel wool. Minimize the pressure, as the wool can cut through the final layer of finish. As a final step, apply a coating of Trewax, a rather good paste wax. The wax not only adds protection to the shellac finish but it also tends to dull the gloss affect that shellac produces. Using a clean rag, rotate the piece on the lathe and polish.

If you were finishing a music box using the above process, you would repeat the same procedures with the lid. As you will discover, the lid can be finished on either a chuck or a screw-center, whichever was used for turning it. The base of the lid as with the box or bowl must be finished off-lathe. You can use the same procedures but they must be done by hand rather than on the lathe.

To obtain a French polish—after the surface has been built up with the solvent-shellac mixture—pour a small amount of 3-pound cut shellac into a separate, dish-type, container. Add a few drops of boiled linseed oil to the shellac and, using a rag, apply a small quantity of the mixture to a portion of the piece to be finished. *Do only a small portion of the surface at a time*. With the lathe running, apply a rag to the area of application but use firmer pressure. While applying pressure, also move the rag over the entire surface very slowly. Allow a drying period between coats, and repeat this portion approach until the entire surface has been done.

For each additional application of shellac, still using the portion approach, add a few more drops of linseed oil to the shellac. Continue the process, using 4/0 steel wool between coatings, until you achieve the type of finish desired. Trewax is also recommended as a final finish for this method; I use it because it has more carnauba wax in it than most other commercially available paste waxes. It is a high-quality wax but also reasonably priced.

As discussed earlier, after the shellac and wax process has been completed on music boxes or bowls, you will still need to turn out the base of the unit. After turning, as described in later chapters, the base section of the box or bowl, you will need to finish this area. This is an off-lathe process that must be done with care.

Assuming the surface of the base or lid has been adequately prepared with abrasive papers, apply the alcohol-solvent mixture and allow to dry. You must be extremely careful that the liquid does not run over to the already-finished surface. After drying, follow each coat with a steel wool treatment as described earlier. Eventually move to the 3-pound cut and the appropriate procedures for it. If desired, a buffing disc on an electric drill or motor can be used for polishing between coats and also for the final wax treatment.

One of the major disadvantages of the shellac finish is that it is not the most durable surface finish—thus the need to apply wax as a final coating. Shellac is not tolerant of water, detergents, and many other chemicals. I have found, too, that it is significantly affected by a lot of handling, although others may have had different experiences with shellac finishes, especially the French polish type. There are other products, for example Deft, that are more durable and can also be applied on-lathe. They represent another group of on-lathe surface finishes generally called the lacquers.

The lacquers, as with shellac, are quick-drying finishes and thus lend themselves to on-lathe finishing methods. They are also nonpenetrating surface-type finishes that need to be built up with multiple applications. While there are many different types of lacquers available that can give wood gloss, semigloss, or a flat finish, I have regularly used the product Deft. It is a semigloss lacquer and it is quite easy to use and maintain.

As with many products, its continued use has become more a matter of habit and familiarity than anything necessarily intrinsic to the product itself. I have used Deft for many years and have been generally satisfied with its performance. I'm also certain that there are other lacquers of equal or better quality on the market with which I am not familiar. As in most areas of finishing, the products used are usually a matter of what you, the finisher, prefer.

In on-lathe finishing, Deft should be used full strength from the can. Many other lacquers can be thinned, or cut, with lacquer thinners to speed their drying time. In general, the finishing methods with lacquers are essentially the same as with shellac. They do, however, build up more quickly and, if you are not careful, they tend to dry unevenly while the piece is rotating on the lathe; a certain amount of experimentation is mandatory.

After applying a coat of lacquer with a brush or rag, turn on the lathe and allow the piece to rotate for a few seconds, As with shellac, be careful of the lacquer that will be hurled off as the piece rotates. While still rotating, apply a clean rag to the entire surface. The rag and rotation, as explained, will generate friction to speed the drying process. The rag also assists in assuring uniformity of the lacquer on the surface in addition to polishing and hardening the finish.

Prior to the application of additional coats, check the label directions for suggested drying time between coats. When sufficiently dry, use 4/0 steel wool on the surface with the lathe rotating. Do not apply too much pressure or you will cut through the freshly dried finish. Be certain to clean off the steel hairs prior to application of another coat.

As indicated, unlike shellac, Deft and other lacquers require substantially more drying time between coats. While friction of the rag speeds the drying process and thus reduces the time between coats, you should still let the piece dry for an hour or two. This time lag is the major drawback to on-lathe finishing with nonpenetrating materials. It tends to tie up the tool and the faceplate for extended periods of time. You may want to figure some short cuts as you develop your own methods of finishing.

Deft, and many other lacquers, will produce a water-and-chemical-resistant finish after some four or five coats. It's usually a durable finish for pieces that will be handled frequently, as, for example, music boxes. Nevertheless, I always complete the process and maintain the finish with a paste wax.

One final on-lathe surface-type finish that can be used is a wax process. In addition to Trewax, you can also use Butcher's Wax or Johnson's Paste Wax for this finish. It's best to purchase the clear or natural-colored wax. Prior to application of the wax to the rotating surface, you should seal the wood. If regular sanding sealer is not available, you can use the alcohol-shellac mixture in its place. The wood must be sealed prior to application of any wax, otherwise it will not properly build up on the surface. After applying a few coats of sealer, carefully apply extra-fine abrasive paper to the surface. This removes the wood hairs and also prepares the surface to hold the wax better. Clean the surface thoroughly following use of abrasives.

The actual application of the wax and use of a rag is the same as for the shellac process. Do not, however, use steel wool or abrasive papers between coats. Their use would totally remove the wax coating. After each application of wax, apply considerable pressure to the surface with a rag. Be careful that you do not generate too much friction or burning will result. Continue to add coats and polish until the desired finish is achieved.

As you will discover, the wax process makes for an extremely attractive finish. Unfortunately, it is not a very durable finish and necessitates continued maintenance. It may lend itself to some of the larger music boxes that would have minimal handling. Again the decision is a matter of choice on the part of the turner-finisher.

In his book *Woodturning Techniques*, W. J. Wooldridge describes his finishing process using carnauba wax. As you may know, carnauba is the hardest of all waxes and is the primary ingredient in most quality paste waxes. While more expensive than the paste waxes, carnauba is available from a number of finishing suppliers and may be well worth trying. You can either use carnauba in its solid form, as it comes from the supplier, or liquify it with xylene or naptha. It's definitely a process to try at some point if you enjoy wax-look finishes.

There are other products, both penetrating and nonpenetrating, that can be used as on-lathe finishes, and those mentioned are only a few that I have used on music boxes. Also, there are any number of alternative methods and techniques to apply finishing products when using an on-lathe method. Experiment with your own methods and ideas, in addition to suggestions in books among the references. It's frequently helpful and informative, too, especially with nonpenetrating finishes, to seek the counsel of other turners or woodworkers using them.

Off-Lathe Finishes

Music boxes and bowls lend themselves to off-lathe finishing methods. In that I enjoy hand-finishing each piece, this dictates a preference for off-lathe finishes. An added consideration is that I generally prefer a less glossy finish than what the on-lathe methods create. Also, I prefer being able to finish the entire piece at a more leisurely pace than is allowed in on-lathe finishing, and off-lathe methods do not tie up the tool and the faceplates.

Prior to any finishing, it is necessary to complete the turning process and preparation of the surfaces. As you will note later, I often drill all the holes in the base sounding board of the musical units before finishing them. When lids are involved, they too are completely ready for total finishing. As I prefer finishing a number of pieces at one time, the off-lathe methods lend themselves to how my shop operates.

While on occasion I use only a penetrating-type finish, more often I use a combination of both penetrating and nonpenetrating finishes. In that oils tend to bring out and sharpen the grain and figure of the wood, I always use a penetrating finish first. I prefer the oil look of the wood but, with music boxes and bowls, I also recognize the need for a surface finish as well. By the nature of how music boxes are used, it is almost mandatory that a surface finish be applied both for protection and for ease of maintenance.

As the penetrating finish of choice, I always use Watco Danish Oil (natural). I've tried any number of other products but have been most satisfied with the Watco. In addition to its high quality in its enhancement and protection of woods, it's extremely simple to use. On pieces that may be used for holding food, I usually use Watco Danish because, when dry, it is nontoxic. Another excellent nontoxic finish is Behlen's "Salad Bowl Finish."

Prior to using Watco, or any product, be certain you read the label. When ready, I line up a series of pieces to be finished on newspaper on the floor of the shop or outside. In addition to rags and a container to hold a portion of oil for application, I also have a few pieces of 600-grit wet/dry silicon carbide paper handy. Using a small rag dipped in the Watco, I wipe on a liberal portion all over each of the pieces. After letting the oil soak in for a few minutes, I lightly move the abrasive paper over the surface, with the grain. This process removes the tiny hairs that are raised by the oil and also assures good distribution of the oil on the surface. After about fifteen minutes, using a clean soft rag, I wipe the remaining oil off the surface. Since the oil will sometimes liquefy the print on newspaper, you must be careful that ink does not adhere to the surface of the piece being finished. If you prefer, use scraps of pine on which to place the freshly oiled pieces for drying. I usually let the oil dry for at least an hour.

When I plan to have only a penetrating finish on a piece, I give it a second coating of Watco oil. I allow it to sit for at least an hour before wiping the remaining oil from the surface. Other than allowing it to dry thoroughly, and occasionally wiping off any excess oil that may surface, the piece is finished. I rarely put wax on after oiling, but if you want the wax effect allow the piece to dry for at least twenty-four hours.

For most music boxes and bowls I use only one application of Watco oil. The oil enhances and beautifies the wood and this appearance will remain. After at least twenty-four hours, I use Deft, the nonpenetrating lacquer, for the balance of the finishing process. Along with Deft, I use the reliable 4/0 steel wool method and often a final coating of paste wax.

In applying Deft I use a brush and cover all surfaces with the exception of the base ridge on the music boxes and bowls. Similarly, I Deft the knob and top of the lid but not the bottom. This allows the placement of the pieces on wooden blocks until dry. I finish the base edges and bottoms of the lids last. Normally I apply three coats of Deft, allowing ample drying time; after each coat is dry, I rub the surface very carefully with 4/0 steel wool. This tends to remove any dust or other particles that may have attached themselves to the surface. The wool also tends to dull the appearance of the Deft and give the surface a less-coated look. If desired, you can apply a final coat of paste wax and polish it. The use of wax is a good way to maintain the finish of the piece.

This combination off-lathe approach has been very satisfactory for me. It is not only easy but it leaves the piece with a good woody appearance. The finish has also proved to be very functional for music boxes and bowls that are subject to a great deal of handling. However, as with most finishers, I continue to try new products and methods, always looking for the ideal. I encourage you to do the same.

References

Blandford, Percy W., *The Woodturner's Bible*. Blue Ridge Summit, PA: Tab Books, 1979.

Child, Peter, *The Craftsman Woodturner*. London: G. Bell & Son, 1971.

Ensinger, Earl W., *Problems in Artistic Wood Turning*. Woburn, MA: Woodcraft Supply Corp., 1978.

Ernest, Scott, *Working in Wood*. NY: G. P. Putnam's Sons, 1980.

Fine Woodworking. Bimonthly publication, Newtown, CT: Taunton Press.

Fine Woodworking Biennial Design Book. Newtown, CT: Taunton Press, 1977.

Fine Woodworking Techniques, vols. 1,2,3. Newtown, CT: Taunton Press, 1978, 1980, 1981.

Frank, George, *Adventures in Wood Finishing*. Newtown, CT: Taunton Press, 1981.

Gibbia, S.W., *Wood: Finishing and Refinishing*, 3rd ed. NY: Van Nostrand Reinhold, 1981.

Hall, Allen, and James Heard, *Wood Finishing and Refinishing*. NY: Holt, Rinehart and Winston, 1981.

Hand, Jackson, *How to Do Your Own Wood Finishing*. NY: Harper & Row (Pop Science) 1976.

Hayward, Charles H., *Practical Veneering*. NY: Sterling, 1979.

———, ed., *The Woodworker's Pocket Book*. Englewood Cliffs, NJ: Prentice-Hall, 1982.

Hogbin, Steven, *Wood Turning*. NY: Van Nostrand Reinhold, 1979.

Holtzapffel, John, *Hand or Simple Turning: Principles and Practice*. NY: Dover, 1976.

Meilach, Donna Z., *Creating Small Wood Objects as Functional Sculpture*. NY: Crown, 1976.

———, *Woodworking: The New Wave*. NY: Crown, 1981.

Nish, Dale L., *Artistic Woodturning*. Provo, UT: Brigham Young Univ. Press, 1980.

———, *Creative Woodturning*. Provo, UT: Brigham Young Univ. Press, 1975.

Nilsson, Ake R., *Woodware*. NY: Drake, 1976.

Pain, F., *The Practical Wood Turner*. NY: Drake, 1974.

Seale, Roland, *Practical Designs for Wood Turning*. NY: Sterling, 1979.

Stokes, Gordon, *Beginner's Guide to Wood Turning*. London: Pelham Books, 1974.

———, *Woodturning for Pleasure*. Englewood Cliffs, NJ: Prentice-Hall, 1980.

Thorlin, Anders, *Ideas for Woodturning*. Englewood Cliffs, NJ: Prentice-Hall, 1980.

Wooldridge, W.J., Woodturning Techniques. NY: Sterling, 1982.

The Block
Music Box

Chapter 3

THE BLOCK MUSIC BOX

The block music box design is one that can be used with a wide variety of woods. While the degree of turning skill required is less than in other music box or bowl designs, some of the block designs require rather high-risk turning behaviors. As you will be working with a square object on a chuck, extreme caution must be exercised with the block boxes in their various shapes. This is especially true if you decide to turn a block that, by the nature of the wood, must be turned with a portion of it off-center. As will be discussed, you will probably want to reduce the lathe speed and also move the tailstock into place to add a measure of security. I make a practice of wearing leather gloves when turning and, very often, a safety shield over the face. If your lathe has a protective shield as part of it, the risk factors are reduced significantly with the exception of your hands. The turner, at least the wise one, will always assess and anticipate the possible hazards of turning a particular piece and prepare accordingly.

One of the interesting things about the block designs is that many different pieces of wood can be used. While the blocks should be at least 1½″ (6/4's) to 1¾″ (7/4's) thick, the thickness requirement is only necessary for that portion of the block where the music movement will be placed. Thus, you can use pieces with bark on an edge (be certain the bark is tight or it will fly off when turned); chunks that contain some crotch or burl but also have a rough edge; pieces that the dealer or sawmill cut off and discarded; split and dried logs from the backyard wood pile.

The block box can also be turned from standard stock that you may have available. I have turned block boxes from most of the popular hardwoods up to 8″ square and 3″ (12/4's) thick. You can also make up specialized boxes using veneer or plugs. Pine 2″ × 4″ studs can also be used if desired. You may want to make your initial box from pine as it's quite easy to turn and inexpensive compared to the hardwoods. When available, I have also turned, as discussed earlier, larger music block boxes from spalted woods. Spalted woods are a bit more of a problem to turn but the end result is well worth the effort. A number of examples in explaining turning musical boxes will use spalted sycamore. The actual size and type of wood employed for the block designs is clearly a matter of preference and availability.

To assist you in turning an initial music box with lid, the following specific (numbered) tasks focus on turning a box 3½″ square and 1¾″ (7/4's) thick. The thickness of the wood is the critical factor because, you will recall, your music movement has fixed dimensions. Assuming you have a Reuge or similar 1/18 music movement, the task for all block designs is to turn a 1″-deep hole with a 2½″ diameter. These dimensions will comfortably house the movement and, for the initial design, will also allow space for a lid with a ⅛″ tenon. With a ½″-deep area turned from the base of the block, the sounding board will be ¼″ thick. Illus. 3-1 is a cutaway that depicts how the first and subsequent designs will look when finished. As will be demonstrated, the first block music box design can be turned on a self-made chuck. While a 3″ faceplate can also be used, and will be recommended on the larger block designs, the chuck is adequate and simpler to use on the smaller units.

Illus. 3-1 Cutaway of Block Music Box

Illus. 3-2 Finished Block Music Boxes

Design 3-1: The Block Music Box with Lid (Illus. 3-2)

1. Cut a 3½″-square block, 1¾″ (7/4's) thick. Mark a center point on the top of the block.

2. Using a pencil compass or circle template, make a 2½″-diameter circle on the block; be sure to clearly mark the center point. Also, make the circle line as dark as possible. If the line is sufficiently dark, it will be a visible guide when the block is rotating on the lathe for turning.

3. Using a ⅛″-diameter drill bit, drill a hole at the center point through the entire block. (It is assumed here that you are using a ¼″-diameter lag screw in your chuck.) The drilled hole must be small enough to provide holding capacity on the chuck screw.

4. After mounting the block on the chuck, align the tool rest and the tailstock (Illus. 3-3). Until you develop confidence in the chuck system, you may want to use the tailstock to secure the block against the chuck. A ball bearing tailstock center is preferable for this procedure. Using a 4″ tool rest will make the turning process much easier.

5. While maintaining the integrity of the 2½″-diameter hole, your initial cut can be with a ½″ or 1″ skew chisel. Thrust the point of the skew in the visible circle line on the surface of the block. Once you have firmly established the circumference of the circle, begin using a ½″ roundnose scraper and a square nose scraper or chisel, about ½″ or ¾″ in size. These tools will allow you to remove the wood and also keep the side wall and, eventually, the bottom face flat. Remember your lag screw from the chuck is protruding through the center of the box. Turn close to it but obviously not into it. As you turn, stop and check the depth of

Illus. 3-3 Block Chuck-mounted for Turning Movement Area

the hole so that you do not exceed 1″. You can remove the pillar of wood that surrounds the lag with a wood chisel after the block has been removed from the chuck (Illus. 3-4). Incidentally, it is normally not necessary to use abrasive papers on the inside wall and bottom of the box after turning. Most of this area will be covered or hidden from view by the musical movement.

6. After removing the block from the chuck, carefully chisel out any excess wood that remains after removing the pillar. A flat bottom is necessary for the placement of the music movement. Also, good contact between the movement base and the wood makes a more effective sounding board.

7. Screw the block back on the chuck, through the turned hole, with the base facing out (Illus. 3-5). The tailstock should be moved into the base for more secure turning.

8. Stopping frequently to check the depth, a hole needs to be turned in the base that is approximately ½″ deep and 2¾″ in diameter (Illus. 3-6). For this procedure, a ½″ skew chisel, a ½″ round-nose, and a 1″ square chisel or scraper are effective. This necessary depth and diameter allows for sufficient space for the movement shaft and turning key with its wings. It allows for ease of winding the movement and also free rotation of the key when the movement is playing. Depending on the original thickness of the wood used (in our design the block was 1¾″ thick), the box bottom or sounding board should be approximately ¼″ thick.

9. Using a circle template or pencil compass, trace a 3¼″-diameter circle for the lid, using stock that is at least ¾″ thick. Mark a center point in the circle on the surface that will be the bottom of the lid. Cut out the lid. The 3¼″ diameter of the circle allows for sufficient wood to be turned off, but also

Illus. 3-4 Wood Pillar Surrounding Lag Screw

Illus. 3-5 Block Chuck-mounted for Turning Base Key Area

Illus. 3-6 Turned Key Area with Lag Screw Pillar

makes possible a ⅜″ or greater lip for the lid to overlap the hole when placed on the box. You may want to review the cutaway in Illus. 3-1 that depicts how the lid with tenon looks when in place. If desired, you may want to use plugs or some other decorative method to enhance the lid. These techniques were presented in our discussion of specialized blocks.

10. Assuming a ¼″ lag screw is in the chuck, drill a ⅛″-diameter hole about ½″ deep into the bottom surface of the lid at the marked center point. The hole is not drilled through the lid block. It needs only to be sufficiently deep to be held on the lag screw of the chuck for turning.

11. Mount the lid block on the chuck. If the base of the lid does not snug-up tight against the face of the chuck, make and use one or more shims for placement on the screw between the chuck face and the lid block. Tighten the lid block firmly against the shim(s).

12. To facilitate turning the lid without slippage or danger of it being hurled off the chuck, use the tailstock center and a small circle of wood (Illus. 3-7). The wood will prevent the tailstock center point from penetrating and thus marking the lid top. The lid can be rough-turned using a ½″ roundnose and a 1″ skew chisel, or tools of choice.

13. Using a vernier caliper, set the outside jaws by snugging the inside jaws against the wall of the turned hole in the box (Illus. 3-8). The outside jaws' setting will be the guide for turning the lid tenon diameter. The tenon is necessary for keeping the lid in place on the box.

14. Remove the tailstock and finish turning and shaping the lid as desired.

15. Using a parting tool, make the lid tenon approximately ⅛″ long and a fraction smaller than the preset outside caliper jaws (Illus. 3-9). Be sure to check the tenon frequently with the preset caliper so you don't cut off too much wood. The lid

Illus. 3-7 Lid Ready for Turning

Illus. 3-8 Measuring Diameter with Vernier Caliper

Illus. 3-9 Cutting Lid Tenon

tenon diameter needs to be a wee bit smaller than the hole diameter. This allows for any expansion of the wood but also makes the lid easier to use. You must also plan and allow for at least a ⅜″ lip on the lid for overlap. For clarification, refer back to Illus. 3-1.

16. After completion of the tenon, finish turning if necessary and use the appropriate abrasive papers to finish the lid. When the tasks are completed, remove the lid from the chuck and test the lid tenon and overlap for fit. If the overlap is too great or the tenon too tight, remount the lid on the chuck and reduce accordingly.

17. Before sanding the base of the lid tenon, fill the drill hole with an appropriately colored wood filler. When dry, sand the lid tenon to final finish.

18. With the exception of sanding and the finishing process, the block box is now complete and ready to receive the initial placement of the music movement. Remove the winding key, place the movement in the box, and, when it is centered on the bottom, carefully press down on the spring barrel housing. This slight pressure will allow the winding stem to make an indentation on the bottom of the box. Using a sharp punch or pencil, locate the indentation and make it more visible.

19. Using a ⅜″ bit, drill a hole where the stem indentation is on the bottom of the box. Drill all the way through the base. A good sharp spur or similar wood bit should be used to avoid splintering.

20. Place the music movement in the box with the winding stem centered in the ⅜″ hole. For this task, you need to hold the music movement in place with one hand while checking the underside of the sounding board. Then, being careful that the movement doesn't slide and thus lose the alignment of the centered stem, place the box down on a firm surface. Use a sharp punch or pencil to mark through the holes in the bedplate of the movement that are to receive the fixing screws.

21. Use a ⅛″-diameter bit to drill the fixing screw holes as marked through the bottom of the sounding board.

22. Using abrasive papers, sand all four sides and the top and bottom of the box. If you have a floor belt sander, the task is rather simple. For appearance, slightly sand off and roll the box edges on both the top and bottom. Do not round off the edges of the hole that will receive the lid tenon. Also, do not put any finish on the box.

23. Place the music movement in the box and secure it with the finishing screws. Screw the

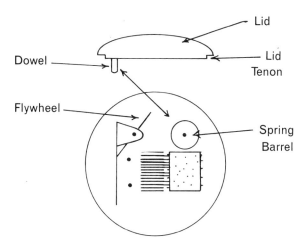

Illus. 3-11 Diagram of Lid On/Off System

movement only when the finish is completely dry. Also, be certain the lid is dry prior to placement on the box. After oiling the movement, place it into the box and secure it with the fixing screws. Apply the tune sheet over the hole in the underside of the sounding board, near the winding key (Illus. 3-10).

24. (Optional method 2) If sliding stoppers or other commercial devices are not available, a lid-dowel system can be made for an on/off mechanism. Illus. 3-11 shows how the system works.

25. Cut a ¾″ piece of ⅛″ doweling. Matching the lid and box grain, mark on the tenon a spot approximately ¼″ in from the edge of the lid tenon.

26. Drill a ⅛″ hole approximately ⅜″ deep at the point marked on the lid tenon. Using a spot of glue, place the dowel piece in the hole and tap. Allow the glue to dry (Illus. 3-12).

27. To test the on/off effectiveness of the dowel, place the lid on the box and turn it so the dowel moves into the flywheel. Wind the movement, turn the lid away from the flywheel without removing it to see if the movement begins to play. By turning the lid, which in turn moves the dowel into and away from the flywheel, the movement should turn

winding key on the shaft, wind the movement (don't overwind) and listen. If the fixing screws have been turned too tightly, the movement may either not play or will play too slowly. If necessary, loosen the screws.

24. (Optional method 1) If a sliding stopper—for example, a Reuge weighted stopper (P 717)—is to be used, the box is complete. Before applying any finish, remove the movement. Replace the

Illus. 3-12 Lid Tenon About To Receive On/Off Dowel

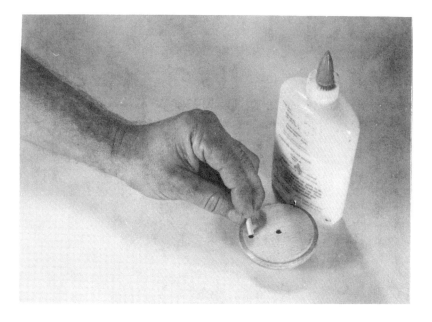

on and off. If the system does not work, remove, by sanding or cutting, a portion of the dowel. Repeat the process until the system works efficiently. The movement can, of course, also be turned on by simply removing the lid.

28. If desired, no on/off mechanism is neces- sary. Many prefer to simply wind the movement and allow it to play without interruption.

29. Finish the box and lid as desired. Reassemble the movement into the box, place the tune sheet over the hole under the sounding board and enjoy the clockwork sound.

Design 3-2: Block Music Box with Glass Insert (A) (Illus. 3-13)

As pictured, this block design is larger than the previous unit and does not utilize a lid. The design calls for the use of a round glass insert placed on a shoulder over the musical movement. Unless a commercial stopper mechanism is available to control the on/off modes of the movement, this design does not lend itself to an inconspicuous, self-made device. An alternative on/off mechanism that I have employed with this design will be presented for your consideration. You may decide to use the dowel system discussed or simply to operate the movement without any control mechanism at all.

The format of tasks and figures used in presenting Design 3-1 will be used in this section and throughout subsequent presentations. Where there is exact duplication of tasks, in some instances, you will be referred to an early presentation. Also, as this design requires a glass insert, I detail the procedures for cutting glass circles. That instruction should serve as a reference for other boxes and bowls that necessitate similar

Illus. 3-13 Large Square Spalted Sycamore Music Box

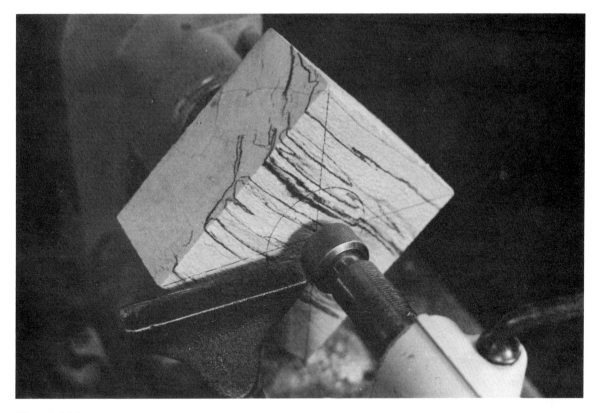

Illus. 3-14 Large Block Faceplate-mounted for Turning Movement Area

glass covers. A block of spalted sycamore is used to demonstrate Design 3-2, but any wood of sufficient thickness and width is appropriate for the design. Two optional methods, the faceplate and chuck, are presented for your consideration. The faceplate method will be used to demonstrate the initial task in the design.

1. Cut a 5"-square block that is at least 1¾" (7/4's) thick. Using a ruler, determine and mark a center point on the top and, if a faceplate is to be used, also mark the center of the bottom.

2. Using a pencil compass or circle template, make a 2½"-diameter circle on the top surface of the block. This marks the area that will be removed to house the movement. If the line is sufficiently dark, it will be a visible guide when the block is rotating.

3. (Optional method 1) If a short chuck is to be used, drill a ⅛"-diameter hole through the entire block at the center point. This hole must be smaller than the diameter of the lag screw for good holding capacity.

3. (Optional method 2) If a faceplate is to be used, carefully center the plate, using your base center point, and attach it to the block using appropriately long wood screws. When using a faceplate with this design, do not drill a hole through the box at this point. That task will be done later, when appropriate.

4. Whether using a chuck or faceplate, mount the block on the lathe, move the tailstock into place, and align a small tool rest (Illus. 3-14).

5. With larger blocks it is wise to reduce the speed of the lathe down to 1475 or 990 rpm, or in that general range. This is largely a safety consideration and should be done in relation to the various speed capacities of your lathe. If the wood is turning too roughly, which happens at slower

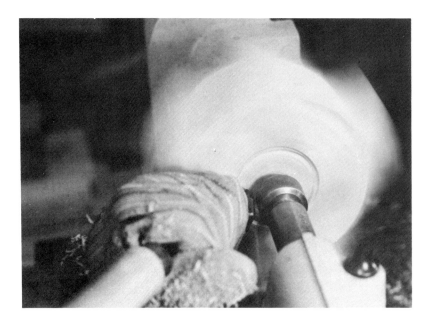

Illus. 3-15 Initial Tool Cut in Block Surface

speeds, you may want to increase the speed a bit. I definitely recommend wearing a leather glove on your hand nearest the block. Remember, this is a rotating square with sharp edges that can really hurt; I know from experience. Be very careful when doing square blocks or off-center turning.

6. To maintain the integrity of the 2½″-diameter hole, I initially use a 1″ skew chisel to cut along the premarked circle on the face of the block (Illus. 3-15). The balance of the turning, if using a faceplate, can be done with a ½″ roundnose scraper and a ½″ square nose chisel or, if desired, a ¾″ square nose scraper. The square noses are used to keep the walls straight and also to make a flat clean base. I usually move the tailstock away and mount a larger tool rest when the hole is about ½″ to ¾″ deep. If a chuck is used, leave a pillar of wood around the lag screws and remove it later with a wood chisel. When a chuck is used, the tailstock can also be removed when it is time to finish the walls and most of the base. With a ¼″-diameter lag screw on the chuck and penetrating through the base of the block, I usually have a pillar with about a ⅜″ diameter. This normally provides sufficient holding power and it permits finishing most of the inside base.

The actual depth of the 2½″-diameter hole is determined by the thickness of the block used. You must plan for the dimensional requirements. For example, you must allow at least ½″ for the winding key area underneath the block and also ¼″ for the sounding board. As a glass insert will be used, an additional ⅛″ must be allowed for that. The ⅛″ allows for sanding the top surface of the box, plus sufficient thickness for the glass insert and shoulder. I explain shortly how the shoulder is made to hold the insert. It should also be remembered that you need a minium of ⅞″ depth for housing the musical movement. In the spalted sycamore 1¾″ (7/4's)-thick block that is being used to demonstrate this design, the 2½″-diameter hole, allowing for the above dimensional requirements, should be 1″ deep. In this situation, especially when using a spalted wood, you may want to make the glass-insert shoulder a bit deeper to allow for more surface to be sanded away. If this were done, you would still have sufficient depth for the movement. These are the kinds of dimensional considerations and figurings that go with turning musical boxes and bowls.

7. If the block is being turned on a faceplate, a small indentation must be made at the precise

center of the inside base of the hole just turned. This mark will serve as the point of entry for a ⅛″-diameter hole that will be drilled through the block for the next step in the turning process. To make this indentation, turn on the lathe and use a 1″ skew chisel. Place the point firmly against the bottom of the box at the approximate center and the tool and lathe will do the rest. You only need a very small hole in the exact center, so that when the hole is drilled and the block is mounted on the chuck it will not be off-center. If you used a chuck for the initial turning, you are already prepared for the next turning task.

8. Before removing the block from the lathe, it is necessary to cut the shoulder where the glass insert will rest. I use a ½″ square nose chisel for making the shoulder. The shoulder should be at least ⅛″ wide and ⅛″ deep. As suggested, the thickness of the block may offer some flexibility

with the depth. With wood that requires minimal surface sanding on the top of the box, your shoulder needs to be only a fraction larger than the thickness of the glass insert; the glass I usually use is about ³⁄₃₂″ thick. When cutting the shoulder, be sure the tool used is sharp. I carefully align the tool and eyeball the approximate ⅛″ width and then lightly place the tool on the surface to make the shoulder. In that I have standardized a number of these dimensions to precut glass inserts, I use an insert to check the accuracy of the width and depth of the shoulder. The ideal, when finished cutting the shoulder, is to have the glass insert and the top surface almost flush. The excess wood usually is removed when sanding the top surface of the block (Illus. 3-16).

9. If a faceplate is being used, remove the faceplate and drill the ⅛″-diameter hole through the box at the premade indentation on the inside base.

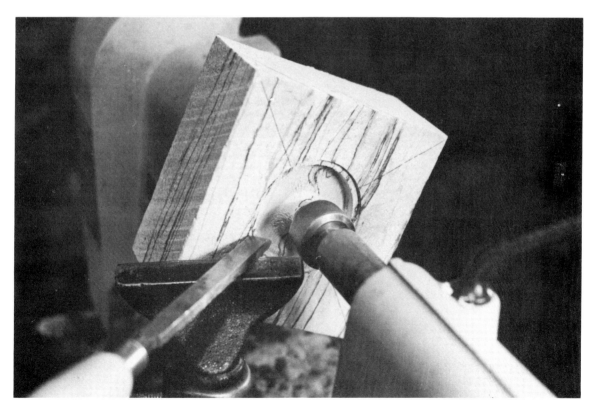

Illus. 3-16 Glass-insert Shoulder

10. Using the long chuck mounted on the lathe, screw the block through the 2½″-diameter hole, using the lag screw. Snug the block tight to the surface of the chuck. Bring forward the tailstock and align the tool rest (Illus. 3-17).

11. For turning the base area that will house the winding key and tune sheet, use a ½″ skew chisel, a ½″ roundnose scraper, and either a square nose chisel or scraper. This area should have a diameter of at least 2¾″; it must be wider than the movement hole because of the wings on the winding key. If the area is not sufficiently wide, the wings of the key will hit the side walls of the base and not allow the movement to function. The depth of this area should be at least ½″ and, if your previous measurements were accurate, that

would leave a sounding board of ¼″ thickness (Illus. 3-18). Remember, when turning, to allow a pillar to develop around the lag screw. The pillar can be removed later with a wood chisel.

12. With the exception of sanding and finishing, the box is now ready for the initial placement of the musical movement. The movement, with the key removed, should be centered in the 2½″-diameter hole. After it is centered, carefully press down on the spring barrel housing to force the winding stem to make a mark on the sounding board surface. Locate the mark left by the movement winding shaft and, using a punch or pencil, make it more visible.

13. Using a ⅜″ bit, drill a hole through the box at the point of the stem mark. This hole, of course,

Illus. 3-17 Large Block Chuck-mounted to Turn Base Key Area

Illus. 3-18 Base Key Area Turned

will be where the winding stem will penetrate the base area of the box. Use a good sharp wood bit to ensure a clean hole.

14. Place the movement in the box with the winding stem in the exact center of its hole. The movement must be centered in the box but, equally important, the winding shaft must also be centered in its hole. After the alignment of the entire movement, holding it firmly in place, turn the box over and center the winding stem most exactly. This can be rather tricky but it's critical that it be done correctly. When the stem is aligned, holding the movement firmly in place, turn the box upright and carefully set it down. Using a sharp punch or a pencil, mark through the holes on the movement's bedplate that will receive the fixing screws.

15. Drill the fixing screw holes, as marked, through the sounding board with a ⅛″ drill bit. A sharp bit is recommended to prevent splintering.

16. To sand the large square blocks, I generally use a 6″ × 48″ belt sander with a 120-grit belt. With spalted woods, I use a 100-grit to begin the sanding process. After bringing all surfaces to the desired finish, you may want to roll the edges on both the top and bottom surfaces. This tends to give the piece a more finished look. You can also sand the sharp edges off the inside edge of the key housing area in the base. Do not sand the sharp edges of the insert area or the inside shoulder. You may want to smooth the top edge of the 2½″-diameter hole but do not roll it.

17. While you may prefer to purchase your glass inserts, my preference is to cut my own. In addi-

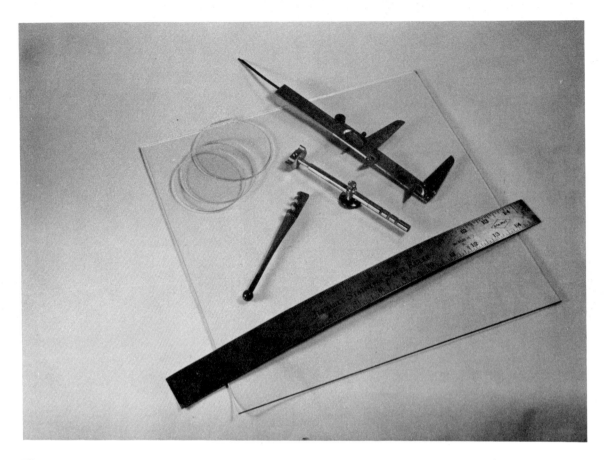

Illus. 3-19 Devices Necessary for Cutting Glass Inserts

tion to the glass, you need a vernier caliper, a ruler, a standard glass cutter, and a circle glass cutter (Illus. 3-19).

18. With the vernier caliper, establish the exact inside diameter of the glass insert area. If you are unable to read the caliper, place the preset jaws on the ruler to determine the exact diameter of the insert required. Next, with the circle glass cutter placed on the ruler, set and lock it at exactly one-half the diameter of the insert area. The cutter is set at one-half the diameter because it is located and revolving from the midpoint of the circle when it is cutting the glass. If there is a suction cup system on the circle cutter, place a little saliva all around the edges of the rubber suction cup. Place the cup on the glass, and press it down to activate its holding capacity.

It's best to plan your cut on the glass sheet as near to the edge(s) as you can. With your left thumb (if you're right-handed) firmly placed over the suction cup, use your right hand to move the cutter head over the glass. Put pressure on the cutter that is sufficient to let the cutter wheel scratch the glass surface (Illus. 3-20). It's somewhat tricky at first to make the total circle cut without the cup slipping or some other frustration occurring. After a few attempts, however, you should master the procedure.

After the circle has been scratched with the cutter on the glass, use the weighted end of the standard glass cutter to tap the glass just outside the circle cut. It's best to do this over a wastebasket to catch the glass as it falls away. If sharp edges remain on the insert, use the appropriate-

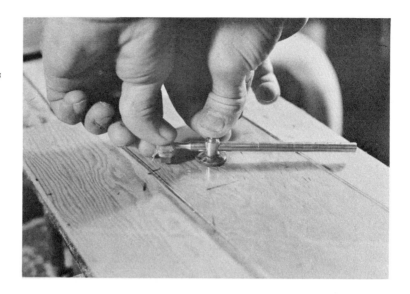

Illus. 3-20 Ready to Cut Glass Insert

sized chipping groove on the back side of the standard cutter. Be careful when chipping so that you don't break the insert. I recommend using a face mask whenever working with glass; very small sharp threads of glass tend to fly off when tapping or chipping.

I have found in cutting glass that you must be somewhat aggressive with it. If your cutter is sharp and the wheel oiled lightly, you can approach the glass and cut it any way you desire. If you're timid in your approach and lack confidence in the cut-

ter, you probably will have problems. Glass is reasonably inexpensive, and if a piece breaks you've only lost a little time; you will, however, have learned something about the glass-cutting process.

A final procedure on glass cutting. As the edge is usually rough after cutting, I tidy it up on the belt sander. With a full face mask and a pair of leather gloves, after activating the belt sander, I place the edge of the insert on the belt (Illus. 3-21). I very slowly rotate the insert in the op-

Illus. 3-21 Cleaning Glass-insert Edges on Belt Sander

posite direction to the moving belt, applying only a small amount of pressure. You will note, if the glass is allowed to remain in one position for too long, it will turn red from friction and begin to melt in that area. After a number of complete turns of the insert against the belt, the edge is usually clean and shiny. This method is also useful if you cut your insert too large; it's a good way to reduce the size of the insert. Use caution with this procedure, and be sure that you hold the insert tightly. The gloves will protect your hands from the glass and also from the heat that is generated.

If a frosted effect is desired on the surface edges of the insert, this too can be accomplished on the belt sander (Illus. 3-22). Simply rotate the insert, allowing the surface edges on both sides of the glass to rub against the sanding belt. Be careful that only the very edges of the surface touch the belt or it will scratch the surface.

After the glass insert has been prepared to your satisfaction, test it for fit in the shoulder area of the block box. If it's too large, as suggested just above, reduce its size on the belt sander. If it's too small, begin the process of cutting a new insert. By all means handle your insert with care until it is glued into place in the finished box. In subsequent projects where you may use glass inserts in musical boxes and bowls, refer back to this discussion of procedures as necessary.

19. The block box can now be finished as desired. It obviously will require an off-lathe type of finishing process.

20. When the block is sufficiently dry, place the

Illus. 3-22 Frosting Glass-insert Edges on Belt Sander

Illus. 3-23
Diagram of Large
Block On/Off
System: Top View

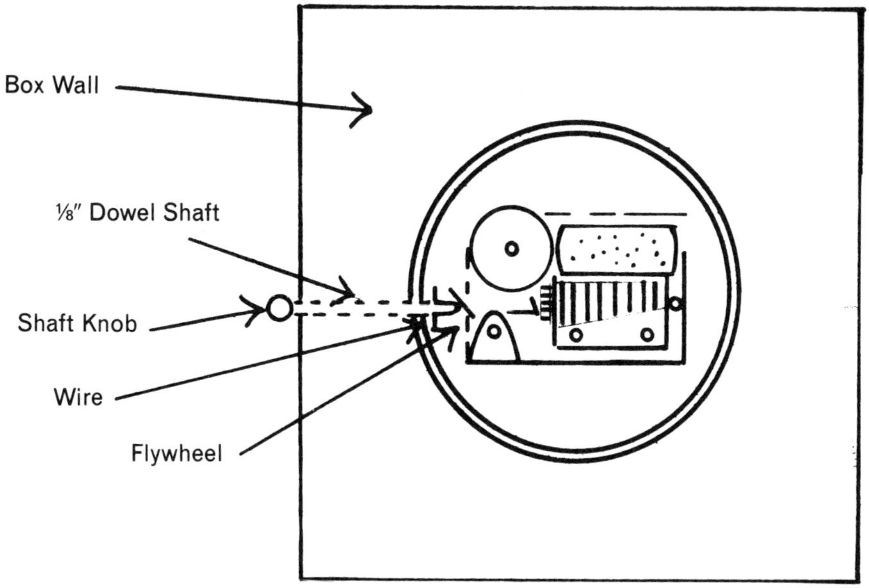

Box Wall

⅛" Dowel Shaft

Shaft Knob

Wire

Flywheel

music movement in the base and secure it with the fixing screws. You may want to oil the appropriate points of the movement prior to placement in the box. After securing the movement, wind it and test it to be sure it's functioning properly. If it runs too slowly, loosen the fixing screws. On occasion, as discussed earlier, if the base is not perfectly flat, the screws, when tightened, tend to affect the gear mechanism.

21. (Optional on/off mechanism) Prior to placement of the glass insert, you may want to make an on/off system from a small dowel. It is certainly not necessary, but it does offer an interesting control option if you do not have commercial stoppers. Illus. 3-23 details how the system works. The mechanism requires a ⅛" dowel at least 3" long, a ⅛" high-speed drill bit, and a small piece of very thin wire. As you note on the diagram, the dowel penetrates the wall of the box directly into the path of the flywheel. Operationally, as the dowel is pulled away from the flywheel, the mechanism begins to play. As the shaft is moved into the flywheel, the movement stops. To assure accuracy in placement of the dowel, measure down the inside wall to that point which is in direct alignment with the flywheel. Transfer, precisely, this mea-

surement to the outer wall and mark. This will give you the point for drilling a hole and eventual insertion of the dowel through the wall. Remove the movement prior to drilling to prevent hitting it with the bit and also to keep sawdust out of its mechanism.

If a high-speed bit is to be used, make a slight indentation with a nail or punch at the mark on the outside wall. This will prevent your drill bit from "skating" along the surface of the box wall. After drilling through the wall with the ⅛" bit, leaving the bit still in place in the hole, widen the hole very slightly with the edge of the bit. This very slight enlargement of the hole will permit free movement of the dowel without it being sloppy in the hole. Obviously, the alternative option is to use a drill bit that is fractionally larger than the ⅛" dowel shaft.

Before cutting the dowel to an appropriate length, replace the movement in the box and secure it. Place the dowel through the hole to be sure that it strikes the flywheel. Move the dowel back and forth in the hole to be sure that it does not bind. If there is binding, widen the hole a fraction. Then determine the length the dowel needs to be for movement into the flywheel, but

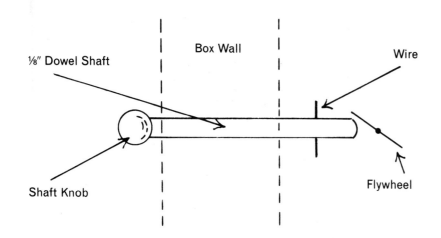

⅛″ Dowel Shaft

Box Wall

Wire

Shaft Knob

Flywheel

Illus. 3-24 Diagram of Large Block On/Off Dowel Shaft: Top View

with sufficient length beyond the outside wall to grasp it for pulling away from the flywheel. It's best to leave at least ¼″ to ⅜″ of dowel extending from the outside wall. That length will accommodate a small knob or ball that you may want to make to secure the outer end of the dowel. The knob will not only make the dowel easier to grasp but will also prevent it from dropping into the movement area.

After determining the appropriate length of the dowel, cut off the excess. To prevent the complete withdrawal of the dowel from the hole when turning on the movement, a small piece of wire can be placed either through the dowel or around it. Illus. 3-24 shows how the dowel should look when completed. Before placing the dowel through the wall in its permanent position, you may want to

put paste wax on the shaft. Place the dowel through the wall, insert the wire and, to be certain it remains secure, place a drop of white glue on it and the dowel. If the movement has been properly oiled, secure the fixing screws and test the total system.

22. To glue the glass insert in the shoulder, use white glue and a toothpick. Place a few small drops of glue on the edge of the insert and place it on the shoulder. Do not use too much glue as it tends to squeeze out on the underside of the glass and look rather unsightly. Also, you may want to remove the glass at some point in the future so don't overglue.

23. The final step is to place the tune sheet in the center of the key area. As indicated, I generally place it over the chuck screw hole in the base.

Design 3-3: Block Music Box with Glass Insert (B) (Illus. 3-25)

As the photo indicates, this design is essentially the same as Design 3-2. The major difference between the two designs is the type of block used. Also, the nature of an unbalanced block, especially when it has sharp edges or bark, presents the turner with some high-risk turning. The blocks, even though the faceplate is dimensionally centered, have uneven weight distribution. Thus,

in turning, the block will rotate very much like a planned off-center piece. Definitely wear gloves and a full face mask while turning. With this type of block, a faceplate should initially be used, along with the tailstock, and run the lathe, initially, at about 990 rpm.

As the steps for turning this block design are essentially the same as for the previous one, you

Illus. 3-25 Finished Walnut Block Music Box

should refer to that section for most of the tasks required. There are, however, a number of tasks that are sufficiently different to need some explanation.

After finding a chuck of wood that lends itself to this type of block design, you must make some decisions about the dimensions desired. Illus. 3-26 shows a rough-cut block from a discarded piece of walnut. The block is approximately 4½″ square and 3″ (12/4's) thick and is ideally suited to this type of design. You should plan a block to dimensions in part dictated by the wood, but also by the size music box desired. The dimensions, within the limits of the rough edge(s), should be

Illus. 3-26 Rough Walnut Block

approximately equal on all four sides. On occasion this is not possible because of the nature of the block and a rough edge. You may want to retain a larger portion of the rough edge because of its beauty. It frequently is worth doing that, especially if it's an exceptionally attractive edge.

1. Cut a block to the desired dimensions. In the example shown in Illus. 3-26, as stated, the block is approximately 4½″ square and 3″ (12/4's) thick.

2. Using a ruler, determine the exact center of both the top and bottom surfaces of the block. On the top surface, using a template or pencil compass and the midpoint as a pivot, draw a 2½″-diameter circle. On the base surface, if a 3″ faceplate is to be used, draw a 3″ circle for use in aligning the plate when mounted to the block (Illus. 3-27).

3. Attach the faceplate on the base surface within the circumference of the circle. A faceplate rather than a chuck is recommended for the initial turning stages of this design. The faceplate provides greater holding power and thus more security for the turner.

4. Mount the assembly on the lathe, bringing the tailstock forward and aligning the tool rest. Be sure to reduce the speed of the lathe before the turning begins. Remember, also, to wear appropriate safety gear.

The remaining tasks for this design are essentially the same as outlined for Design 3-2. If desired, you may use the through-the-wall-dowel on/off system as previously described.

As you begin exploring the possibilities for other block music box designs, you will be

Illus. 3-27 Laying Out Block for Turning

amazed at the innumerable options. For example, a triangle design can be used, as can any number of other geometric shapes. Special blocks can be prepared to utilize veneer, plugs, or laminated woods. With almost any block design a lid can be planned and turned, if desired. The immediately preceding three designs are only samples that suggest possibilities for different music box turnings. I encourage you to explore and put into effect some of your own ideas.

Music Boxes
with Lids

Chapter 4

MUSIC BOXES WITH LIDS

While it is, for many, something of a misnomer to refer to a round container as a box, it is, in fact, simpler and in some ways more descriptive. There are round boxes but most of our life experience has been with square ones. Similarly, when thinking about music boxes, we generally think in terms of squares or rectangles. No doubt this tendency also prevented the early music box craftsmen from developing round boxes.

My initial interest in musical boxes emerged from turning round boxes with lids. The round container is not only a natural housing for the musical movement but it is strikingly different in terms of most people's experience. In examining my music boxes, most people are amazed to discover a musical movement in a round container; music boxes are supposed to be square or rectangular, at least according to their prior experience with them. It is often difficult for people to accept the reality of a round music box. These reactions, of course, make the turned object that contains a movement even more of a source of fascination.

The music box design presented in this chapter is a rather common design used by most woodturners. There is nothing especially innovative about it other than that it is tooled to house a music movement. Since some may not have turned boxes with lids, I detail the procedures that I use

when making them. While there is some duplication of instructions between the several designs that are presented, it is done to minimize reference to earlier material. On the other hand, where the remaining tasks for a design seem obvious, and typical to turning any music box or bowl, the instructions are terminated. Where a special task—for example, cutting glass inserts—has been discussed earlier, the instructions will not be repeated.

In general, the box designs presented represent four different sizes of boxes with lids. While the turner can experiment with the basic box designs, it is the lids that provide the greatest opportunity for creative turning. The box designs all lend themselves to using almost any wood available or desired. As a minimum, however, you will need stock that is at least 2″ (8/4's) thick; the first design uses wood of that thickness. You will find, as you turn more music boxes and also use different manufacturers' movements, that you can use thinner stock for some boxes. Initially, however, it is worth turning your first boxes with lids from wood at least 2″ (8/4's) thick. I use glass inserts in the designs presented, but they are optional. I also use different stopping mechanisms; one system that can be crafted by the turner is presented. As you will soon note, the box designs each allow for a storage area in the box.

Design 4-1: Music Box with Lid (Illus. 4-1)

This design is a rather standard-looking box with lid; almost any wood is acceptable for it. In addition to a glass insert resting on a shoulder, a disc can also be turned to cover the edge of the glass.

This is strictly a decorative touch. One optional method for a stopping system will also be presented. Lids for this design can either be turned from stock that is about 1″ (4/4's) thick or you can

Illus. 4-1 Finished Music Boxes with Lids

desired, the design lends itself to using plugs or veneer. You may want to prepare a special block to use for this first design.

The design is most easily turned using both a faceplate and a chuck. While it is possible to turn the entire project with a chuck, I am inclined to use a small faceplate during the initial turning tasks. If you prefer on-lathe finishing, this design lends itself to these methods; also, the lid can be finished on the lathe if desired. The wood used for this initial example is walnut.

1. Using stock that is at least 2″ (8/4's) thick, trace a circle with a 3½″ diameter. Either a pencil compass or circle template simplifies this task and also permits marking the center. The circle and center point should be made on what will be the top surface of the block. (The midpoint is only necessary if you plan to turn the entire unit on one of the short chucks described earlier. That is the point where you would drill a ⅛″-diameter hole through the block to receive the chuck lag screw.)

2. If a band saw is available, cut the block along the premarked circle lines.

3. Attach a 3″ faceplate on the block, using ½″ wood screws. If you do not have a faceplate that small, prepare and use a gluing block as dis-

glue up a special block that includes a knob. The example given includes a knob piece for the lid. Preparations for specialized blocks for lids and boxes were discussed in an early chapter. Also, if

Illus. 4-2 Faceplate-mounted Block Ready to Turn

Illus. 4-3 Turning Outer Wall of Box

cussed earlier. The other option is, of course, the small chuck.

4. With wood that is approximately ¾″ (3/4's) thick, using a pencil compass or template, make a 3½″-diameter circle for the lid. Also, trace a 1¼″-diameter circle on the same stock for a knob block.

5. Cut out the lid and knob circle blocks. Sand the top surface of the lid and the bottom surface of the knob block in preparation for gluing. Using a yellow glue, assemble and clamp the lid and knob. Watch for slippage from alignment as a result of the glue and clamp. Allow the assembly to dry according to the glue instructions.

6. Mount the box block and the faceplate on the lathe. Move the tailstock with a ball-bearing center forward and align a large tool rest parallel to the block (Illus. 4-2).

7. With a lathe speed of about 2220 rpm, turn the outside of the box. I often use a ½″ roundnose and a heavy-duty scraper for turning the box. This design utilizes a straight outside wall; you can, when using a larger block, be more creative in your turning (Illus. 4-3). Do not turn off any more wood than necessary, as you will need a turned diameter of about 3⅛″.

8. Using abrasive papers, bring the wall to a finishing-ready surface. As previously discussed, move from the course grits to at least a 220-grit or finer paper. Work especially hard on the cross-grain areas if necessary. Often they tend to look "mousey" unless the box was turned with a deep gouge or was carefully sanded. It sometimes helps, when using abrasive papers, to move the paper diagonally across the surface. This tends to cut off the wood hairs rather than forcing them back down into their natural setting. When doing this or, for that matter, any sanding, do not use too much pressure. You would be well advised to use a piece of carpeting pad or similar material as a sanding block. If you have a drum switch on your lathe, reverse the rotation of the motor and apply your abrasive to the surface. When finish-sanded, apply 4/0 steel wool to the surface.

9. Leaving the tailstock in place, align a 4″ tool rest near the top surface of the block. The next turning task is to cut a shoulder for the lid, another for a glass insert or possible on/off system and begin the process of turning the inside of the box. It is assumed that your box has a least a 3⅛″ finished diameter.

10. Using a square nose scraper or chisel, clean

Illus. 4-4 Initial Turning on Top Surface of Box

and square the top surface of the box up to the tailstock center.

11. The initial cut into the surface should be for the lid shoulder. With a ½″ skew chisel, using the point, cut a ⅛″-deep trench exactly 3⁄16″ from the outer edge of the box wall. Using a roundnose scraper, remove about ¼″ of wood from the trench working towards the center of the box (Illus. 4-4).

12. With a ½″ square chisel, cut the lid shoulder from the 3⁄16″-wide lip at the top edge of the box. The shoulder should be approximately 1⁄16″-deep and ⅛″ wide. This leaves an outer-wall ridge of 1⁄16″ (Illus. 4-5). To cut the shoulder, be certain the chisel is very sharp. After marking, or, if you can approximate the necessary dimensions, simply force the chisel straight into the surface to make the shoulder cut. Since the lid will be turned to fit the shoulder, these shoulder dimensions can be somewhat rough.

13. In addition to the lid shoulder, you must also plan for the glass-insert shoulder. This design has a storage area over the insert. The thickness or dimensions that you must allow for with a 2″ (8/4's) box are: the base winding key area, approximately ½″; sounding board base, ¼″; musical

Illus. 4-5 Lid Shoulder Turned

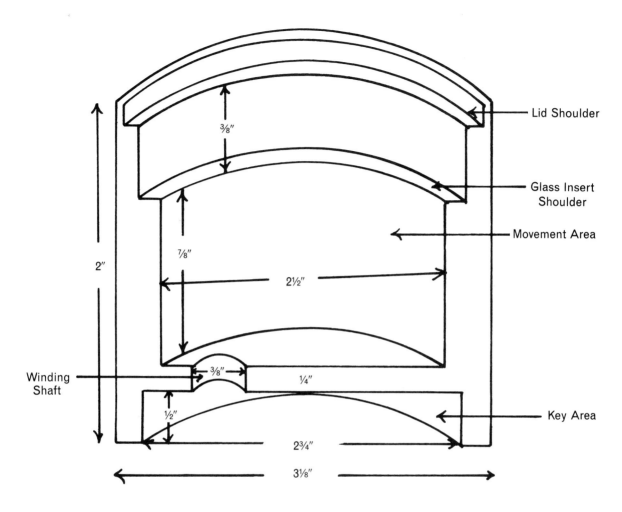

Lid Shoulder

Glass Insert Shoulder

Movement Area

3/8″

7/8″

2″

2½″

Winding Shaft

3/8″

¼″

Key Area

½″

2¾″

3⅛″

Illus. 4-6 Diagram of Music Box: Cutaway

movement area, ⅞″. These fixed dimensions, for this specific block, leave an area of approximately ⅜″ for the glass insert, a ¹⁄₁₆″ disc to cover the insert edge, storage, and the lid shoulder. It should be remembered that the box has a finished diameter of 3⅛″, which is more than adequate to allow for the lid and insert shoulder and still have a 2½″ diameter for the center to house the movement (Illus. 4-6).

You will find that frequently the winding key area can be reduced to a ⅜″ depth and thus provide an additional ⅛″ for the storage area. The required space is determined by the length of the winding stem and the key shaft. These lengths, if

you remember, vary among manufacturers. Again, you need to plan your final dimensional needs for the box based on the type of musical movement that will be used.

14. Remove the tailstock and, with a roundnose or similar tool, remove wood from the center area of the box to a depth of 1¼″. On a 2″-thick box, this would leave a ¼″ sounding board and a ½″ key area in the base. With a ½″ or larger square nose chisel or scraper, cut the inside wall straight, beginning at the edge of the lid shoulder. Cut the wall straight, in a 2″ (8/4's)-thick box, to a depth of ⅜″ and make the glass-insert shoulder. This insert area should be approximately ⅛″ wide. From the

Illus. 4-7 Inside the Turned Music Box

inside edge of the insert shoulder, cut the wall straight to the sounding board. This should be a depth of at least ⅞″ from the insert edge. Using a square nose, make the sounding board surface flat and clean. With a 1″ skew chisel, place the point at the approximate center of the sounding board and, with the lathe running, let the point make a small indentation at the midpoint. This is where a hole will be drilled to allow the block to be screwed on the lag screw of the chuck (Illus. 4-7).

15. Using fine abrasive paper, lightly sand the top ridge of the box. This upper edge is part of the outer box wall and will be highly visible when the lid is in place. Be careful not to sand off too much of the surface. Unless desired, the inside area of the box does not require sanding. If desired, the box is now ready for on-lathe finishing methods.

16. Remove the assembly from the lathe, take off the faceplate, and drill a ⅛″-diameter hole through the base of the box. Use the indentation on the sounding board surface as the point of entry for the bit.

17. With the long self-made chuck mounted on the lathe, screw the box on the lag screw, bring forward the tailstock, and align the small tool rest (Illus. 4-8).

18. The base key area needs to be approximately 2¾″ wide and ½″ deep. A ½″ skew chisel works well for cutting into the surface for the outer edge of the area. Remember the lag screw is extending through a portion of the center of the base. You must allow a pillar of wood to surround it. Clean out the key area using a ½″ roundnose and a square nose chisel or scraper (Illus. 4-9). Lightly clean up any roughness on the bottom of the outer wall of this area. Using abrasives, you may want to finish the outer and inner edge of this wall while you have the opportunity. If you finished the outer wall of the box by on-lathe finishing methods, you may also want to finish the base edge and part of the key area at this point.

19. Remove the box from the chuck and, carefully, using a wood chisel, remove the pillar that surrounded the lag screw. With the chisel, carefully level and clean the area where the pillar was attached.

Illus. 4-8 Box Chuck-mounted for Turning Base Key Area

Illus. 4-9 Box Base Key Area Turned

20. The next task is to turn the lid and its knob, assuming the glue is dry. Mark the midpoint on the base of the lid and drill a ⅛″-diameter hole approximately ½″ deep. This hole is for screwing the lid block onto the small self-made chuck for turning.

21. Using the small chuck mounted on the lathe or, if desired, a screw-center with a shim, mount the lid assembly. Bring the tailstock forward and align the tool rest for turning the lid base (Illus. 4-10).

22. With a vernier caliper, determine the exact

Illus. 4-10 Lid Chuck-mounted Ready to Turn

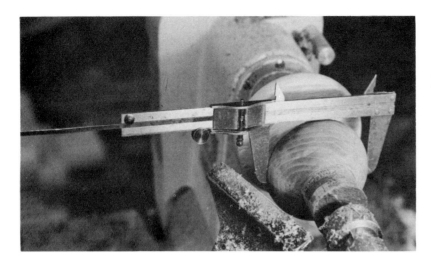

diameter of the box lid area, so setting the outside jaws. This diameter will be essentially the same for the base of the lid.

23. Using a ½″ roundnose scraper, turn the base edge and the top portion of the lid. Periodically check the base area with the preset vernier caliper. The lid should be a fraction smaller than the preset measurement; this makes for a better-fitting lid base and also allows for any possible expansion of the wood. Be careful that you do not turn off too much wood from the lid

base or it will have to be done over again (Illus. 4-11).

24. Align a small tool rest to turn the box knob. The tool rest should permit turning from the base of the knob where it attaches to the lid surface to the top edge of the knob. Be certain to leave the tailstock in place. Turn the knob and lid area using a ½″ roundnose or any tool that would be appropriate for a planned knob design (Illus. 4-12).

25. Remove the tailstock and align a tool rest to

116

Illus. 4-13 Turned Top of Knob

turn the top surface of the knob. As there is an indentation in the surface from the tailstock center point, I usually turn a cup in the knob top with a ½″ roundnose. Do not use too much pressure as you could break the knob shaft (Illus. 4-13).

26. With various grits of abrasive paper, sand the lid and knob while still mounted on the chuck and lathe. Bring the surface to a finishing readiness. After sanding and prior to finishing, remove the lid and test it for fit in the box. If it is too tight, replace it on the chuck and bring the surface down to dimension. If you are using on-lathe finishing methods, you can now finish the lid and knob but, obviously, not the base.

27. Remove the lid from the chuck and, before sanding, fill the screw hole in the base with an appropriately colored wood filler and allow to dry. Sand the base to its finished surface.

28. With the winding key removed, place and center the music movement in the base of the box. After it is aligned, press on the spring barrel to allow the winding shaft to make a small mark on the sounding board surface. Remove the movement and, with a pencil or punch, make the shaft mark more visible.

29. Using a ⅜″ bit, preferably a spur bit, drill a hole through the sounding board at the point just marked on the surface.

30. Place the movement in the box, centering it and also the winding shaft in the ⅜″ hole. While holding the movement firmly in place, turn the box over to be certain that the winding shaft is perfectly centered in the ⅜″ hole. Holding the movement in place, carefully set down the box on a flat surface. Be sure the movement, and thus the shaft, does not move out of alignment. This is a rather awkward but necessary procedure.

31. With the movement perfectly aligned in the box, using a pencil or sharp punch, mark through the fixing screw holes on the bedplate to the surface of the sounding board. Drill fixing screw holes through the base, using a ⅛″ drill bit.

32. Place the movement in the box, secure it with the fixing screws, wind (don't overwind) and test the movement. Sometimes, if the screws have been turned too tight, the movement tends to play rather slowly. If necessary, loosen the screws.

33. If an on/off mechanism is not to be used, cut and prepare the glass insert for the box. Refer to the detailed instructions regarding cutting and finishing glass inserts in the previous chapter. If you plan to make the suggested on/off mechanism,

Illus. 4-14 Decorative Disc and Block

do not cut a glass insert; instead refer to Optional method 2 (40) below.

34. A decorative disc can be made to fit over the edge of the glass insert. If such a disc is used, there is no need to finish the edge of the glass insert because it will be covered by the disc. The disc, which is hollow, should be made from the same wood as used in the box proper. Illus. 4-14 shows a finished disc and the block from which it was cut.

35. To turn the insert disc, attach a small face-plate to a block that is 1″ (4/4's) or larger in thickness. The block should be cut round with a diameter that is at least ¼″ larger than the inside diameter of the finished box. Thus, in our example, the block should have a diameter of approximately 3⅛″. Place the assembly on the lathe, move the tailstock forward and align the tool rest. The vernier caliper's outside jaws should be set based on having determined the inside diameter of the box. Using appropriate tools, turn the block to shape and dimension, checking frequently with the caliper. It is best to turn the block a bit smaller than the preset caliper jaws indicate. There is no need to sand the wall of the block as the disc edge is not visible when in place (Illus. 4-15).

36. Align the tool rest in front of the block after having moved the tailstock out of the way. It is necessary to tool the top surface of the block square and clean. Using a ½″ skew chisel, with the point make a cut ⅛″ in from the outside wall of the block. The disc should be at least ⅛″ wide,

Illus. 4-15 Checking Diameter on Disc Block

Illus. 4-16 Inside of Disc Block Being Turned

38. Since the discs are very fragile, handle them with care. Depending on the type of band saw blade used, you may or may not have to sand the top surface of the disc. I usually lightly sand the inside edges of the disc with 220-grit abrasive paper. Place the finished disc in the box over the glass insert to check for fit.

39. If the disc is too large, using the long self-made chuck mounted on the lathe, slide the disc on the chuck shaft. Do not force it beyond its diameter or it will split. To prevent the disc from sliding down the tapered shaft of the chuck, wrap some masking tape around the chuck surface next to the disc. With the lathe on, carefully apply 150-grit abrasive paper to the disc's edge and reduce it to the required size. This procedure necessitates a

thus this cut. With a ½″ roundnose for removing wood and a square nose for making the inside walls straight, prepare an area inside the block that is at least ⅜″ deep (Illus. 4-16). I generally prepare discs only as I need them but, as a rule, I make two discs of the same size. When finished, the discs are quite fragile and, on occasion, they are broken. I save the turned block and mark it accordingly for future disc needs.

37. Remove the disc block from the lathe and leave the faceplate attached. If available, using a fence, set up a band saw to cut the discs approximately ³⁄₁₆″ thick. The faceplate can be firmly gripped in one hand, forcing the block surface into the fence. Using a push stick, move the assembly into the saw and cut two discs (Illus. 4-17).

Illus. 4-17 Cutting Decorative Discs on Band Saw

great deal of care or you will break the disc. If it does break, frequently it can be glued together and used. Test the disc for fit, and apply finishing material when appropriate (Illus. 4-18).

40. (Optional method 1) If a commercial on/off stopper, for example the Reuge weighted stopper pictured earlier, is to be used, the box is almost complete. The glass insert and, if desired, the decorative disc should both have been prepared. If off-lathe finishing methods are to be used, remove the musical movement and replace it only when the finish is totally dry. Before final placement of the movement in the box, oil the movement at the appropriate points that were identified earlier. After securing the movement with the fixing screws, apply the tune sheet over the hole in the underside of the sounding board, near the winding key.

Before placing the glass insert in place, be sure to clean it carefully, especially the bottom side. When clean, using white glue and a toothpick, place a few drops of glue on the edge of the glass and set it in place on the insert shoulder. Do not use too much glue. If a decorative disc has been prepared for use, follow the same gluing procedures with it. Allow both to dry. Often it is necessary to weight both the glass and the disc down

while the glue is drying. You should now have a functioning musical box with lid to enjoy.

40. (Optional method 2) A self-made on/off system can be designed if desired, although it is not necessary to have any on/off mechanism on a musical box. The self-made system is essentially a solid disc with a dowel that penetrates it and rests on the glass-insert shoulder (Illus. 4-19). If this system is used, a glass insert is not to be used. To make the on/off solid disc, cut a circle that is at

Illus. 4-19 On/Off Solid Disc and Dowel System

120

Illus. 4-20 Disc Chuck-mounted for Turning

least ¼″ wider than the diameter of the inside of the box. The disc, when finished, should be approximately ⅛″ thick. Before turning the disc to the required diameter, the thickness of the circle can be reduced by ripping it on the band saw. When the disc has been prepared using the above procedures, drill a ⅛″ hole exactly in the center. Using either the short chuck or the screw-center mounted on the lathe, screw the disc on the lag. To hold the disc in place when turning, using a small

block, drill a ⅛″ hole through it and screw on the lag and snug it against the disc face. If necessary, because of slippage on the part of the disc, use another block together with the tailstock to apply pressure (Illus. 4-20). Turn the disc using a ½″ roundnose or some other appropriate tool. Check the diameter frequently using the preset caliper. The disc should be turned a fraction smaller than demanded by the caliper. This allows the disc to move more freely when in place on the insert shoulder. When the disc is finished, remove it from the lathe and check it in the box for proper fit. If it is too large, replace it on the lag and reduce to size. When the process is complete, sand smooth both surfaces of the disc. Do not fill the drill hole in the center of the disc as it can serve as an opening for the clockwork sound to escape.

Cut a 1″ piece of ⅛″-diameter dowel. The on/off system works by having the dowel move into and away from the flywheel of the movement. There is also a small portion of the dowel that should extend through the top surface of the disc, which piece permits the rotation of the entire disc and thus the lower portion of the dowel with a finger, into and away from the flywheel (Illus. 4-21). Drill a ⅛″ hole through the disc approximately ⅜″ in

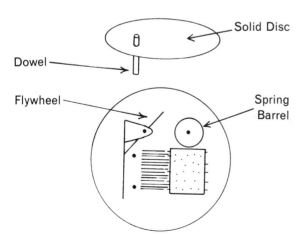

Illus. 4-21 Diagram of On/Off Solid Disc and Dowel System

from the edge of the disc. This measurement is only appropriate for a box where the movement area has a 2½″ diameter. (For other box diameters, specific dimensions and the location of the dowel over the flywheel must be determined.) Place the dowel from top to bottom through the hole in the disc. The dowel should penetrate only to the top edge of the flywheel. Wind the movement and test the system, using a finger, by rotating the disc-and-dowel into and away from the flywheel. If the system works, place a drop of white glue on the

dowel and underside of the disc. Allow the glue to dry and then trim the excess dowel extending up from the disc surface to a length of about ¼″. As a final touch, lightly sand the edges of the dowel ends round.

Remove the movement and, using off-lathe methods, finish the box, lid, and disc. Oil the movement and secure it in the box with fixing screws. Apply the tune sheet over the drill hole in the key area of the box, screw on the key, and the unit is ready for use.

Design 4-2: Music Box with Lid (Illus. 4-22)

As the photo indicates, this design is similar to the previous unit. The differences that are significant between the two are the size of the box, the lid, and the knob. This design offers substantially more storage area inside the box. Also, it affords the turner more wood, especially on the lid and

knob, for some creative turning. As with the previous design, this unit employs both the glass insert and the decorative disc. If commercial stoppers are not available, you may want to forgo an on/off system with this design. Because of the depth of the storage area and the size of the unit,

Illus. 4-22 Finished Music Boxes with Lids

Illus. 4-23 Box and Lid Blocks Ready for Turning

having the movement visible through the glass insert greatly enhances the piece.

As you will discover, the dimensional requirements dictated by the musical movement, the glass insert, and lid are essentially the same as in Design 4-1. The significant measurement differences are in the lid and knob thickness, plus an enlarged storage area.

You may want to prepare specialized blocks for the box, lid, and knob of this design. With air dried (AD) wood that has checked, I will sometimes use the veneer process to salvage a block for this unit. The box and lid also lend themselves to the use of plugs. You should definitely try some of your own design ideas with this unit because it provides sufficient wood for innovation.

I initially turn the box, both the inside and outside, using a faceplate, and then move to a long chuck for turning the key area in the base. The chuck is also most effective for turning the lid with the long knob, but I use the short chuck for the lid. Definitely use the tailstock when turning the lid and knob. Because of its length, if the knob isn't supported while being turned, frequently it will either break or turn off-center. This design also lends itself to on-lathe finishing. You may want to try the shellac method discussed earlier.

In that the turning tasks and other procedures are the same as in Design 4-1, you may refer to the various steps presented in that section. It would be a great deal more fun simply to proceed on your own and, if necessary, check on some specific task. I suspect, if you allow yourself the opportunity, you could problem-solve the tasks and procedures more efficiently than merely following directions.

For this box design, I generally use stock that is 2¾″ (11/4's) thick. The circle block for the box should have a rough diameter of at least 3½″. With this width and thickness, you should have a storage area in the box that is at least ⅞″ deep and 2¾″ wide. For the lid, I use stock that is 1¾″ (7/4's) thick. The diameter of the lid circle should be the same as for the rough box, 3½″. The knob is cut from the same stock as the block for the lid. Thus, in this case, the knob should have a diameter of 1¼″ and a thickness of 1¾″ (7/4's). Illus. 4-23 is a photo of the rough box block and lid with the knob, ready for turning.

The turning tools to use for this design are essentially the same as with most music boxes. Most wood removal is done with a ½″ roundnose chisel, sharp cuts are made with a ½″ skew chisel or a ½″ square chisel, the box wall on the outside is cleaned with an extra-large skew scraper, and square nose chisels or scrapers are used for making a straight inside wall and the shoulders. You may very well find other tools more suitable.

Illus. 4-24 Finished Music Boxes with Lids

Design 4-3: Music Box with Lid (Illus. 4-24)

This large box design involves many of the essentials of the previous units. It is made from a substantially larger block of wood, however, and requires a number of different tasks based on specific dimensions. While the unit utilizes a glass insert, it has a trench storage area around the insert rather than above it. This design does not use a decorative disc over the glass insert, so greater care must be taken in cutting and finishing the glass. As with the previous movement, if a commercial stopper is not available, one should probably not be made. If it is mandatory to have an on/off system, the through-the-wall system presented with Design 3-2 of the block music box can be used. Or you may want to utilize the dowel-disc system presented for Design 4-1 of the music box

with lid. If these systems do not meet your needs, I would encourage you to design and develop one of your own. There are many alternative systems that could be developed.

If you have large blocks that may not lend themselves to solid projects, you could laminate them for this design. Both veneer and plugs from different woods could enhance the large box, its lid, or knob. If you do not care to prepare specialized blocks, you may want to draw your own design for this unit. A considerable amount of wood is involved in it, and you may want to be more creative in your turning than the examples presented allow. Some pencil-and-paper design work can be a most productive way to proceed, especially when anticipating turning from a larger block.

As with the previous box-with-lid designs, this unit can be turned completely on a chuck. Generally, however, I prefer using a small faceplate for the initial turning tasks. Since I use screws with the faceplate that rarely penetrate more than ½″ into the base, screw holes are seldom a problem. As you will recall, the base of the box is turned out for the winding key area—which, in most instances, takes care of the screw holes from the faceplate.

Design 4-3 lends itself to an on-lathe finishing process if this is your preference. Both the box and lid, with the exception of their base areas, are lathe-mounted at those points in the process when finishes could be applied. You may want to think about using the on-lathe finishing methods and plan accordingly.

As many of the procedures are the same for this design as for previous ones, the basic steps will be described, but without the accompanying photographs. When a picture seems necessary to clarify a specific task, it will be included. Walnut will be used to demonstrate this design.

1. Using stock that is at least 2¼″ (9/4's) thick, trace a circle that has a 5″ diameter. If you plan to veneer the block, follow the necessary procedures before cutting the block to its round dimension. As suggested, this will greatly simplify the veneering process, especially the clamping.

2. If a band saw is available, cut the block along the premarked circle line.

3. After carefully centering it on the bottom of the block, attach a 3″-or-larger faceplate. If necessary or desired, you can also use the glue block method and then attach the faceplate.

4. With wood that is at least 1⅛″ thick, make a 5″-diameter circle block for the lid. For the knob, because this design lends itself to a long one, use the same block stock that the box circle was cut from. With a diameter of 1¼″, pattern and cut the knob circle from the 2¼″ (9/4's) stock.

5. Before gluing and clamping the knob block to the lid surface, be sure to sand both gluing surfaces for good contact. Using yellow glue, assemble and clamp (Illus. 4-25). Be certain to allow sufficient time for the glue to dry before beginning to turn.

6. Mount the box block and faceplate on the

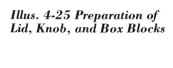
Illus. 4-25 Preparation of Lid, Knob, and Box Blocks

Illus. 4-26 Turning Top Surface of Box Block

lathe with the tailstock forward and the tool rest properly aligned. With a lathe speed of about 2220 rpm, turn the outside of the box. As with previous turnings, use a ½″ or 1″ roundnose scraper together with a heavy-duty skew scraper. With this design, I tend to turn the bottom edge of the wall a bit round. After tooling the surface as desired, finish it with appropriate abrasive papers.

7. With the tailstock remaining in place, align a small tool rest near the top surface. Using a skew or square nose tool, clean the surface and bring it to squareness with the wall (Illus. 4-26).

8. The next turning tasks involve cutting the lid shoulder, making the initial cuts for the storage trench and beginning the glass-insert shoulder. Using a ½″ square nose chisel, cut the lid edge

Illus. 4-27 Outer Edge of Lid Shoulder

126

Illus. 4-28 Finished Turned Lid Shoulder

near the outer wall of the box. The edge or ridge that is created should be approximately 1/16″ wide and about 1/8″ deep (Illus. 4-27).

9. Using a 1/2″ skew chisel, with the point make a cut into the surface that is approximately 1/8″ in from the lid edge/ridge. This cut will finish the lid shoulder (Illus. 4-28).

10. With a small ruler, measuring from the tail-stock center that is in place, make a pencil mark on the surface that is 1 5/16″ from the center. Place the pencil on the mark and, by hand, rotate the block. This circle line marks the outer edge of the glass-insert shoulder (Illus. 4-29).

11. Using a 1/2″ square nose chisel, make a cut 1/8″ deep on the inside edge of the circle you just made on the surface. With the same tool, allowing

Illus. 4-29 Making Circle to Glass-insert Diameter

for an insert ridge that is ³⁄₁₆″ wide, make another cut into the surface area that will be the storage trench. These two cuts firmly establish the glass-insert ridge. Be certain that the glass-insert ridge is not higher than the lid ridge or you will have a problem with the lid fitting. I often reduce the glass-insert ridge a shade lower than the lid ridge just to be on the safe side (Illus. 4-30).

12. The next task is to tool the trench storage area, using a ½″ roundnose. Be careful that you do not cut into the lid shoulder or the glass-insert ridge. I usually turn the trench at least 1″ deep. I also leave it with a round bottom to simplify removal of anything that may be stored in the trench (Illus. 4-31).

13. Remove the tailstock and realign the tool rest in front of the box, possibly using a larger rest. The glass-insert area and the center portion that will house the music movement are turned next. The inside diameter of the glass-insert ridge area should be approximately 2⅝″. This diameter allows for a ⅛″ insert shoulder and also a 2½″-diameter area for the movement. Turn the area with the appropriate tools, remembering to cut the insert shoulder. To accommodate most movements, if you recall, you need a depth of at least ⅞″ in the center area. Because of the thickness of the present block, however, you need to turn this area deeper than usual. Allowing for a ½″-deep key area in the base and a ¼″-thick sounding board, your depth for a 2¼″ (9/4's)-thick block would be 1½″. Some of this thickness is lost by

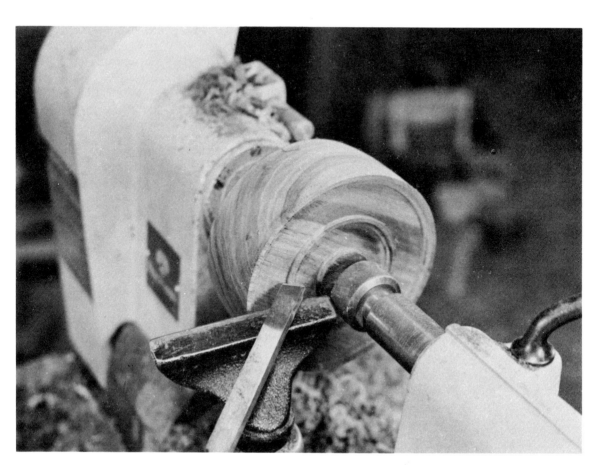

Illus. 4-30 Glass-insert Ridge

Illus. 4-31 Trench-storage Area

cutting the top surface square, and an additional fraction will be removed from the base edge. Nevertheless, you still must turn the hole roughly 1¼″ deep or the sounding board will be too thick. An option is to lower the glass-insert shoulder and ridge to consume a portion of the depth; lowering the glass-insert area gives the box a very interesting effect. In any event, this in one of the dimensional problems encountered in turning music boxes that necessitates some use of your problem-solving skills.

After the walls and sounding board have been squared and finish-turned, make a slight indentation at the exact center of the sounding board surface. This is the point where a ⅛″ hole will be drilled for mounting the block on a chuck. If rough from turning, you may want to sand the trench area. Also, if on-lathe finishing procedures are desired, this is the time to finish the box.

14. After removing the faceplate, drill a ⅛″ hole through the base at the point marked on the sounding board. Using the long chuck, mount the entire assembly on the lathe and bring the tailstock forward. The assembly, after alignment of the tool rest, is now ready for turning out the winding key area in the base.

15. Using a ½″ skew chisel, make the initial cut for the outer edge of the key area. This area should be at least 2¾″ in diameter to allow for the free movement of the winding key. The depth, as indicated, should be at least ½″, which assumes that you solved the problem of the center depth

and have a sounding board that is ¼″ thick. If the sounding board is thicker than that, you can reduce it by making the key area correspondingly deeper. As always, these dimensions are predetermined by the actual length of the winding shaft and key shaft on the movement being used.

Turn the key area as required, remembering to leave a wood pillar around the lag screw that is penetrating through the base (Illus. 4-32). If on-lathe finishing is being used, finish the key area before removing it from the chuck and lathe.

16. After removing the turned box from the chuck, chisel out the lag screw pillar that is attached to the base. Make the area flush with the surface, then sand.

17. Place the movement in the box area, center it, and press down on the spring barrel to mark the key hole spot on the sounding board surface. Drill a ⅜″ hole through the sounding board where marked. Recenter the movement in the box and the winding shaft in the ⅜″ hole. Being careful not

to move the movement and shaft off-center, mark through the bedplate fixing screw holes onto the surface of the sounding board. Remove the movement and drill the holes where marked, to accommodate the fixing screws. Replace the movement in the box, secure it with the screws and test.

18. Cut and finish the glass insert and test it for fit in the appropriate shoulder. If necessary, refer to the glass-cutting instructions detailed in an earlier chapter. This should complete all necessary tasks other than the finishing process, if you're using off-lathe methods.

19. If the glue on the lid-knob assembly is dry, drill a ⅛″ hole in the center of the base of the lid. The hole should be drilled to an approximate depth of ½″; it is for mounting the lid assembly on the short chuck for turning.

20. Mount the lid assembly on the chuck and lathe, move the tailstock forward into the knob, and align the tool rest for turning the lid (Illus. 4-33).

Illus. 4-32 Turned Base Key Area

Illus. 4-33 Lid and Knob Ready for Turning

21. Prior to turning, check the lid diameter required for the box by using the vernier caliper. This setting is needed for turning the base of the lid to the proper diameter. Be sure, when turning, that you periodically check the diameter of the lid with the preset caliper. Test the lid for fit in the box when finished turning.

22. Turn and finish-sand the lid and knob according to your planned design. The top surface and top edge of the knob must be turned very carefully once the tailstock has been removed. Because of its length, the knob can break rather easily. When finished, with abrasive papers and steel wool if using on-lathe finishing methods, apply the necessary finishing products.

23. Remove the lid from the chuck and fill the base lag screw hole with plastic wood or similar material. When dry, sand the base to a finish-ready surface.

24. If off-lathe finishing is to be done, remove the movement and finish the total unit.

25. Oil the movement at the appropriate points, place the mechanism in the box, and secure it with the fixing screws. Test it after winding. Place the tune sheet over the lag screw hole in the key area of the base. Be certain the glass has been cleaned prior to gluing it in the shoulder, then place a few drops of white glue on the edge of the glass and place it in the insert. After the white glue dries, the unit is complete and ready for use.

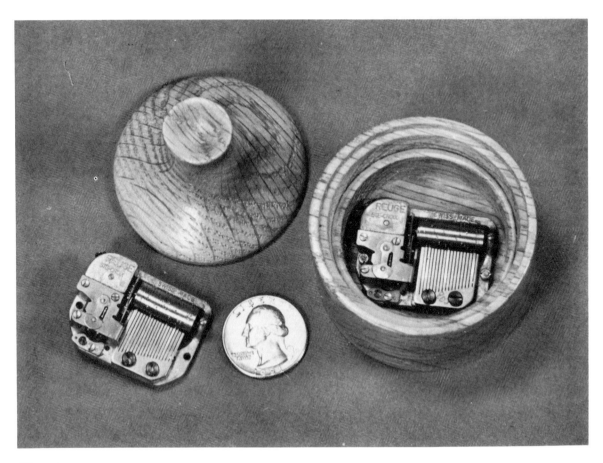

Illus. 4-34 Finished Music Box with Lid and PM Movement

Design 4-4: Music Box with Lid (Illus. 4-34)

In terms of extremes, this design is the smallest of the boxes with lids. Small music movements, at least the quality ones, are quite expensive and often difficult to obtain. Some manufacturers have a line of small movements that you may want to try at some point. Presented in Illus. 4-34 is the Reuge PM 1/18 movement.

This design includes a glass insert over the movement. Additionally, the box has a reasonable amount of storage space for its overall size. The box is turned from stock that is at least 1¾" (7/4's) thick and with a rough diameter of 2½". The lid should be cut from stock that is about ¾" thick

and with the same rough diameter as the box. The knob is cut from the same stock as the lid but should have a diameter of 1".

For turning this design, all procedures are basically the same as for the larger boxes. You must, however, work with a different series of dimensions that are unique to the smaller movements. For example, the area in the box that houses the movement must have a depth of at least ½" and a diameter of 1⅝". The base key area requires at least a ⅜" depth. The difficult fixed dimension with the small movement is for the winding shaft and key. The sounding board can be no thicker than $\frac{1}{16}''$ to accommodate the winding shaft, key, and fixing screws.

Turn this design using a $\frac{1}{2}''$ roundnose, a $\frac{1}{2}''$ skew chisel, and a $\frac{1}{2}''$ square nose. These tools are adequate for any turning task required by the design. Caution must be exercised when cutting and cleaning the sounding board, both on its top and bottom surfaces. Its thinness makes it very vulnerable to breakage.

The box is best turned using a glue block and faceplate. Use paper between the glue block and the box so that they can be split apart easily when necessary. With a $\frac{1}{8}''$ hole through the center of the base, the key area can be turned on a chuck or screw-center. Be sure to use the tailstock for support. The lid and knob can also be turned on the chuck.

With the exception of those considerations mentioned just above, all other tasks are similar to the previous box-with-lid designs.

The Music Box
and Tray

Chapter 5

THE MUSIC BOX AND TRAY

While most lathed music boxes that I've turned have some functional component, i.e., storage area over the movement, early on I became interested in designs that would allow more practicality and usability. As I had turned any number of hardwood serving trays, the linking of the music box with the serving tray seemed a natural combination. The early large box trays also afforded the opportunity to use specific musical-movement tunes in relation to how the piece would be used. For example, the tune "The Entertainer" and other obvious melodies perfectly coordinated the tune with the function of the serving piece. The natural extension of this approach was to design smaller box-tray units for jewelry and similar items; lighter and more romantic tunes were generally housed in these designs. I also experimented with using different woods coordinated to both tunes and designs. It had become clear that frequently the type of wood, the tune, and the design were in conflict. A light cherry box for jewelry, for example, should not house a musical movement that would play Beethoven's *Fifth Symphony*. There is a certain amount of visual and sound dissonance in this kind of combination.

The music-box-and-tray design is simply an extension of two common turning projects, a box with a lid and a serving tray. The significant difference is that the components are glued together to function as a single unit. With the exception of the tray and the key area, once the blocks have been cut and glued, most of the turning tasks are the same as for other music-box-with-lid designs.

In anticipation of turning the box-and-tray de-sign, you may want to review the section on preparation of specialized blocks. Both designs that are detailed will employ these special blocks with no directions for their preparation. You may, as you plan and prepare the box-tray blocks, consider the use of veneer or plugs. As mentioned earlier, I rarely use these decorative touches unless I'm trying to salvage a block of wood. My preferences, however, should not inhibit your own in terms of trying some of these decorative effects. For example, overlapping plugs on a small section of the tray might be rather attractive.

The tasks identified for these designs also assume that the lid and knob have been properly prepared for turning. Similarly, specifics regarding the cutting of a glass insert that should be used in both designs are omitted from the following discussion. If necessary, you should refer back to the detailed presentation on cutting and finishing glass inserts.

Since both designs present considerable wood surface, you may want to use an on-lathe finishing process. You should remember that if the larger tray is planned for use with food, be sure to use a nontoxic finishing product. As with earlier designs, almost the entire unit can be finished on the lathe.

An on/off system is not required for this design. Even though commercial stoppers and self-made systems can be used with either of the units, they're both very effective without them. The opportunity to view the working movement through the glass insert greatly enhances the overall effectiveness of the piece.

Illus. 5-1 Finished Large Music Box and Tray

Design 5-1: The Large Music Box and Tray (Illus. 5-1)

1. The design should have a box with a diameter of at least 3½″ and a thickness of 2¼″ (9/4's) glued to a 9″-diameter tray block. The thickness of the tray block should be at least 1″.

2. Mount a 3″ or larger faceplate, centered at the bottom of the assembly.

3. Place the assembly on the lathe, bring the tailstock forward and align the tool rest to turn the tray edge and base (Illus. 5-2).

4. Using a ½″ or 1″ roundnose, turn the edge of the tray, rolling it towards the bottom. The base area of the tray should be turned up to the faceplate (Illus. 5-3).

5. Realign the tool rest and turn the top surface of the tray. The top area of the tray should be turned so that it has an elevated outer edge. In turning the tray surface, you should also begin rounding the box (Illus. 5-4).

6. Align the tool rest and turn the outer wall of the box to shape. Do not remove too much wood as its finished diameter should be approximately 3⅛″. You need this diameter for the various shoulders and the movement area inside the box (Illus. 5-5).

7. Using abrasive papers from coarse through extra fine, sand the turned surface of both the box and tray. Remember to sand the bottom of the tray up to the faceplate.

8. Lid and knob preparation should be initiated if not already completed. You may want to use a block for the knob that will provide a longer and more interesting one than pictured; my knobs tend to be rather conservative in their design. With a unit of this size, the lid and knob offer the turner an opportunity for some creative turning. You also may want to consider a plug or two; a strip of veneer near the edge of the lid might enhance the piece. Do some designing prior to initiating the preparation of the lid and knob blocks.

9. With the tray-and-box assembly still mounted on the lathe, turn the box center area to include a lid shoulder, a storage area, the glass-

Illus. 5-2 Large Music-box-and-tray Blocks Ready for Turning

Illus. 5-3 Tray Edge and Base Being Turned

Illus. 5-4 Turning Top Area of Tray

Illus. 5-5 Turning Box Wall

insert shoulder, and the space for placement of the musical movement. Be sure to check the dimensions of the movement you plan to use in this design. Remember to allow for a ¼″ sounding board and approximately ½″ for the base key area.

The procedures for turning, as well as the tools, are essentially the same for this box as for those discussed in the previous chapter. I encourage you to work out the process with a minimum of reference to the earlier presentation. You may very well develop a simpler and more effective approach. After the inside area of the box has been turned, you may want to apply your on-lathe finishes. As mentioned earlier, this design has a great deal of surface and thus lends itself to an on-lathe finish.

10. After removing the faceplate and drilling a hole through the base, place the assembly on the long chuck for turning the base key area. Assuming you have planned and turned the box within the dimensional mandates of the movement, this key area is turned the same as on previous designs. *A word of caution with the box-tray design:* Do not make the diameter of the key area too large or you could cut through the tray surface. When the base area has been turned, apply the appropriate finish if on-lathe methods are being used (Illus. 5-6).

11. Using the short chuck, turn the lid to the appropriate diameter and finish-turn the lid-knob unit. If necessary, refer to the earlier discussion of lid-and-knob turning procedures. Apply the finish, if desired.

12. Prepare the glass insert and, if you want, turn a decorative disc to cover the edges of the glass. If off-lathe methods of finishing are used, finish the entire unit. Assuming the necessary holes have been drilled through the sounding board, after oiling, place and secure the musical movement. Apply the tune sheet and screw the key on the winding shaft. After the glass insert and disc have been glued in place, the design is ready for use.

Illus. 5-6 Turning Base Key Area

Illus. 5-7 Finished Small Music Box and Tray

Design 5-2: The Small Music Box and Tray (Illus. 5-7)

1. This smaller unit should have a standard music box with a diameter of 3½″ and a thickness of at least 2¼″ (9/4's). The box, as discussed under special-block preparation, should be glued to a tray block that has a 6″ diameter and is at least 1″ (4/4's) thick.

2. The use of a faceplate is the most effective way to accomplish the initial turning tasks with this design. The long chuck should be used for turning the base key area.

3. After mounting the assembly on the lathe, turn the tray area but focus on making it more of a trench that surrounds the box (Illus. 5-8). The trench can be as deep as your tray block thickness will permit.

4. Finish turning the box and the necessary components on its inside. Remember to carefully measure the musical movement you plan to use so that the various dimensions of the box proper can be turned accurately. After turning, and use of

Illus. 5-8 Turning Trench Area on Tray

appropriate abrasive papers, apply an on-lathe finish if desired.

5. Using the hole drilled through the center of the sounding board, mount the assembly on the long chuck. Turn the base key area to the appropriate thickness and diameter. Finish, if on-lathe methods are being used.

6. Prepare and turn and finish the lid-knob assembly, using the short chuck. Remember to test

the lid base for fit. Also, put plastic wood in the screw hole in the lid base.

7. After the finishing products are completely dry, follow the appropriate procedures for placement and securing of the musical movement. Glue in place the glass insert and, if used, the decorative disc. Place the tune sheet and key in the base area, test the movement, and enjoy.

Design 5-3: The Tray and Music Box (Illus. 5-9)

This design represents the preparation and turning of two separate pieces that can be used together. It is, if you will, a set. The design gives the

woodturner the opportunity to turn a hardwood tray in addition to a music box with lid. I generally turn both pieces from the same type of wood and,

Illus. 5-9 Finished Music Box and Tray: A Set

when possible, from the same stock. Both pieces shown in Illus. 5-9 are turned from walnut.

1. Prepare the tray block using material that is at least 1″ (4/4's) thick and cut to a diameter of roughly 9″. These dimensions are, of course, determined by the size of tray desired. With the smaller music-box-and-lid design, this size tray is proportionately acceptable.

2. It is best to use a glue block with the face-plate in turning the tray. I generally use a pine glue block that is at least 3¼″ in diameter, glued with a paper insert to the center of the bottom of the tray block. The faceplate is a 3″ unit. After the tray has been completely turned, and finished with abrasive papers, I split the glue block from the base and final-finish the bottom surface. If I feel especially adventuresome, I will cut the glue block, using a parting tool, from the tray base. On occasion I will cut through the block and catch the tray with a gloved hand as the two separate. More frequently I cut the block to a shaft with a ¼″ diameter, again using a parting tool, and then cut through the shaft with a hacksaw or similar tool. This process minimizes the finishing tasks on the base. The splitting methods inevitably leave a real mess to be removed.

3. Prepare and turn a music box with lid based on the earlier presentations. Both the tray and the box can be finished on-lathe if you're looking for a glossy finish. Be wary of toxic finishing products if the tray is planned for use with food items.

Illus. 5-10 Finished Musical Serving Bowl

Design 5-4: The Musical Serving Bowl (Illus. 5-10)

This design is an example of the form that musical serving pieces can take. The piece pictured in Illus. 5-10 is from a soft maple block that had been discarded at a sawmill. The finished piece has a 9″ diameter and is 4″ (16/4's) thick. The area that houses the musical movement has a standard box diameter of 3⅛″.

The block from which the piece was turned was severely gouged by a chain saw and also had numerous drying checks. In planning the bowl, these defects were removed to make room for the trench area. The design of the bowl was copied from an angel food cake pan, a rather common item in many kitchens.

Small Music Bowls

Chapter 6

SMALL MUSIC BOWLS

The small bowl designs can be some of the more interesting pieces to turn for housing a musical movement. In many ways, they are also some of the easier designs to craft. One of their advantages is that they can be turned from many different kinds and types of wood. I frequently use blocks that have been cut from the backyard woodpile or some other free source. Pieces that have been salvaged from other shop projects also provide an ongoing source of material. These designs often lend themselves to the use of veneer or plugs, or to laminating with solid woods. You clearly will want to do some design work and prepare some specialized blocks for these small music bowls.

As you will note, it's stretching a point to call some of these designs small bowls. While a few of them have some capacity for storage or for holding items, a number of them do not. They are round like a bowl but there the similarity often ends. Some are simply round pieces that house a musical movement and most stand solely on this function. As you begin designing and turning, you will find that the aesthetics of the wood and music are

sufficient and no other function is necessary or in any way required.

I have sought to present designs that show a number of different approaches in turning small music bowls. While many of the procedures are basically the same as used in earlier designs, some are different; where the differences are significant, they are discussed in detail. On the other hand, for a number of specific details you may want to refer to some of the earlier discussions.

A design feature not included, that you may want to consider, is the use of a lid with knob on some of the flat-top bowls. There will be, as just noted, a number of other design modifications that you may want to implement. And, once again, I hope that the designs presented will pique your own creativeness to initiate different ideas that you may prefer.

Definitely plan to use a glass insert in all the following designs. On/off systems are not necessary unless you have access to the commercial stoppers.

Design 6-1: Small Music Bowl (Illus. 6-1)

1. The three different adaptations of the design in Illus. 6-1 are turned from cherry, soft maple, and spalted sycamore. This design needs a block that is approximately 2½″ (9/4's) thick with a diameter that is roughly 5″.

2. Use a faceplate or, if using a spalted wood, a glue block for the initial turning tasks. Either of these methods provide greater security, especially when turning the spalted woods. The large chuck, as usual, is appropriate for turning the base key area. After completing all necessary tasks, in-

cluding on-lathe finishing, if a glue block is used you may want to separate the bowl from the block using a parting tool.

3. Prior to turning the inner area of the block, be sure that you have checked the dimensional requirements of the music movement. Definitely, you need a glass insert in this design, so plan for and turn a shoulder.

4. As mentioned in Chapter 1 under Woods, when using spalted woods plan to use a great deal of abrasive paper. Frequently you must begin with

Illus. 6-1 Finished Small Music Bowls

a very coarse grit to remove the rotten wood and reach the harder material in the block. Allow ample time for the abrasive process if using spalted wood.

5. In finishing spalted woods, whether using on-lathe or off-lathe finishing methods, definitely use a sealer prior to the application of any surface finishes. The wood, as you will discover, is very much like a sponge when applying finishing products. If a surface finish is planned, be prepared to apply many coats, steel-wooling between each two applications. If other woods are used for this design, the usual finishing procedures apply.

Design 6-2: The Off-center Music Bowl (Illus. 6-2)

Illus. 6-2 Finished Off-center Music Bowl

1. Prepare a circle block that is at least 2¼″ (9/4's) thick and has a diameter of approximately 6″. In the design demonstrated the wood is walnut.

2. Attach a small faceplate at the center of the block base. A faceplate is mandatory for the two major turning tasks required in making an off-center bowl. A long chuck is used, however, to turn the base key area.

3. Mount the block on the lathe and finish-turn the side wall, the bottom edge, and the top surface (Illus. 6-3). The areas should also be finished with abrasive papers. (With this design, I recommend off-lathe finishing.)

Illus. 6-3 Turning Wall on Off-center Bowl

4. Remove the faceplate from the turned block, being careful not to scratch the top surface or the finished wall.

5. What makes this bowl off-center is that the area that will house the music movement is turned near the edge of the block rather than at the center. To accomplish this, the faceplate must be attached directly below the area on the top surface where the movement hole will be turned. The diameter of the movement hole must be sufficient to accommodate the particular type of movement being used. An additional 1/8″ should be added to the diameter to allow for the insert shoulder. Attach the faceplate to the base directly below this planned area (Illus. 6-4).

6. Before mounting the assembly on the lathe, reduce the lathe speed to a maximum 990 rpm or as close as your lathe permits. This is imperative. You must always turn off-center blocks at slower lathe speeds—it's a matter of safety.

Illus. 6-4 Faceplate Alignment on Base

7. Mount the assembly on the lathe and bring the tailstock forward. Align the small tool rest for turning the movement area. With a ruler, measure from the tailstock center approximately 3/4″ on the top surface, and mark. While resting on the tool rest, hold a pencil on the mark and rotate the assembly by hand, thus drawing a 2-1/2″-diameter circle on the block surface (Illus. 6-5). This circle is the outer circumference of the music movement area. After the area has been completely turned out, then cut the shoulder for the glass insert. While you will find that turning is more difficult at the slower speeds required for this design, it is clearly preferable for overall safety. Remember to make a small indentation at the center of the sounding board.

Illus. 6-6 Finished Round Block Music Bowls

8. Following the removal of the faceplate, drill a hole through the sounding board base for mounting on the long chuck. When chuck-mounted, bring the tailstock forward and turn the base key area. Maintain the slow lathe speed.

9. The remaining tasks are typical to the completion of any other musical unit. Check the specific tasks discussed earlier if questions or problems should arise.

Design 6-3: The Round Block Music Bowl (Illus. 6-6)

While obviously not a bowl, the shape and general turning procedures place this design in that gross category. This design is one of many that do not provide any storage space—it is a piece that is designed to perform clockwork music only.

This is a fun piece, easy to prepare and turn. I often try to use scrap materials for this design. One bowl shown in Illus. 6-6, however, is from bocote (cordia). The other bowl is from a block of cherry from the backyard woodpile.

In general, I use blocks that will allow a finished diameter of about 4-1/2″ to 6″. The thickness needs to be in relation to the movement used but, as a general rule, the block should be at least 2″ (8/4's) thick.

Turning can be done using the combination faceplate-chuck approach already outlined. The internal dimensions, including the glass-insert shoulder, are, as always, detemined by the musical movement to be used.

Design 6-4: The Scrap Music Bowl (Illus. 6-7)

As the name suggests, these small bowls are turned from rough scrap pieces. Those in the photo are scraps of osage orange (hedge) fence posts. The design, however, can be used for any

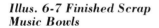
Illus. 6-7 Finished Scrap Music Bowls

153

scrap pieces, especially chucks from the backyard woodpile. As stated earlier, I have a special fondness for wood that is different; while for some these pieces are of no value, I find them to be real treasures and ideal for musical bowls. When the piece does not lend itself for use as a musical container, I often turn the block into a regular small bowl.

Depending on the particular chuck of wood being used, determine whether to use the faceplate directly attached to the block. In some instances it is necessary to use a glue block; on occasion the small chuck or screw-center will also work. Your determination must be based on how the piece lends itself to the various turning procedures. As always, use the long chuck to turn the winding key area.

With pieces of scrap material, carefully examine the block for loose portions that could fly off, or break off from a turning tool. For the initial turning tasks, use the tailstock for support. As you will note in Illus. 6-7, the small scrap bowls all include a glass insert over the musical movement.

Large Music Bowls

Chapter 7

LARGE MUSIC BOWLS

While music boxes and the various small-bowl designs are great fun to turn, none offer the challenge and the satisfaction of the larger musical bowls. Primarily, this has to do with the quantity of wood you're working with on the lathe. Larger blocks allow you many more design possibilities when turning. Also, the wood used for the larger bowls is often replete with the supposed defects that I enjoy the most. When available, the lower-grade hardwoods are generally, from my point of view, the best woods to obtain for turning the larger music bowls.

In many respects I have found the larger music bowls both easier to turn and to finish. Although you are removing substantial quantities of wood from the inside of the bowl, you have more area to work in and can also use the larger turning tools. Issues of dimensions, especially with music movements, are seldom a problem because you have so much space to plan for their placement. For those who enjoy on-lathe finishing, larger bowls offer a real opportunity for some superb finishes.

Most blocks that I use for large music bowls are from 5″ (20/4's) to 6″ (24/4's) thick. On occasion I will obtain some woods that range to 8″ (32/4's) in thickness. Normally I plan for the bowls to have a diameter of from 6″ to 7″. These dimensions are based essentially on the availability of the wood and have little to do with the dimensional requirements of the musical movement. Thus these dimensions are representative of the blocks used for turning most of the large music bowls illustrated in this chapter.

The procedures and tools used in turning the large music bowls are essentially the same as for any other design. Generally, however, I use a ¾″ or 1″ roundnose scraper for most of the shaping of the bowls; I find the larger scrapers more effective and efficient in turning blocks of this size. While on occasion, because it's popular, I turn a bowl with extremely thin walls, my preference is to leave as much wood as possible on the piece. I do not view thinness of walls as especially desirable nor demonstrative of effective turning. It seems a terrible waste of beautiful wood which, by its own growth, is often dense, thick, and heavy.

Because of the size of the blocks to be turned, I always use a faceplate for turning larger musical bowls. I prefer using a 3″ plate because it allows for more shaping at the bottom of the bowl without interference from the faceplate. When turning, as always, I bring the tailstock forward. The long self-made chuck is used for turning the winding key area in the base of the bowl.

The internal dimensions of the bowl are determined by the type of music movement to be used. In most instances you need an area that is approximately 1″ deep and has a 2½″ diameter. The sounding board should be about ¼″ thick unless the winding key shaft necessitates a thinner one. As suggested, measure the length of the winding stem and key shaft to determine the dimensional requirements of the sounding board. Also, allow ½″ of thickness for the depth requirement of the winding key area in the base.

As the bowls, after turning, have a substantial open area above the movement, it is best to plan for a glass insert over the mechanism. This not only will protect the movement but makes for a more interesting piece, so in turning, allow for the cutting of the insert shoulder. I often use a decorative wood disc over the insert. If you do, you must not only prepare the insert but plan for its thickness when cutting the glass-insert shoulder. The preparations for the decorative discs were discussed in an earlier chapter.

Procedures that are typical to placement of the music movement and insert should be followed with the larger bowls. Test the movement and oil it prior to gluing the glass insert and decorative disc in place.

The photos that follow present, with minimal discussion, a series of large musical bowls that I have turned. They are presented to give some idea of designs that I have used in turning larger musical pieces. I hope they will stimulate your own ideas for turning such large musical bowls.

Design 7-1: Osage Orange (Hedge) Music Bowls

The first group of music bowls have been turned from osage orange (hedge) fence posts that were in the ground for many years. The bowls reflect the outer edge of the post, as well as the weathering processes the wood was subjected to over the years. Most of the bowls contain mineral markings from nails that were used to attach barbed wire to the posts. Hedge is an extremely dense wood that dulls turning tools very quickly: it's tough turning but well worth the time and effort. Hedge finishes beautifully.

Illus. 7-1

Illus. 7-2

Illus. 7-3

159

Illus. 7-4

Illus. 7-5

Illus. 7-6

Illus. 7-7

Illus. 7-8

Design 7-2: Walnut Music Bowls

The walnut bowls that are shown have all been turned from air dried (AD) lower-grade hardwood. They represent a few possibilities for large musical bowls that can be achieved with the lower grades of walnut.

Illus. 7-9

Illus. 7-10

Illus. 7-11

Illus. 7-12

Illus. 7-13

Illus. 7-14

Illus. 7-15

Illus. 7-16

Illus. 7-17

Illus. 7-18

Illus. 7-19

Illus. 7-20

Illus. 7-21

The Cranking
Music Box

Chapter 8

THE CRANKING MUSIC BOX

The crank-type movement or manivelle lends itself to turned boxes that can be enjoyed by children and adults. As with other music boxes or bowls, the designs that house the crank movement can be made from any woods. This includes pine.

While I have generally turned three different designs for this movement, they are only a sampling of the possibilities. As these movements are significantly different both in terms of dimensions and method of operation, it is necessary to describe the various steps required in the preparation of the three designs.

You may want to prepare some specialized blocks for use with these designs. All three, including the pine unit, lend themselves to plugs, veneer, or solid laminating.

Design 8-1: The Block Cranking Music Box (Illus. 8-1)

1. Cut a 3½″ square block that is approximately 2″ (8/4's) thick. For this design I frequently use oak.

2. Since this design has no winding key, the dimensional planning is somewhat different. From the base of the movement, measure to the top of

Illus. 8-1 Finished Block Cranking Music Box

Illus. 8-2 Measuring Crank Movement

the unit where the winding shaft enters the mechanism. In a Reuge M 1/18, this height is 1″ (Illus. 8-2). Measure the length of the crank shaft. In the pictured movement this length is approximately ⅝″. The final measurement required is for the base area of the movement. For our sample movement the base is approximately 1⅞″ × 1⅝″. The dimensions are gross measurements but are accurate enough for our purposes. The base dimensions determine the eventual diameter of the movement hole that must be turned from the block.

3. As you plan the box, remember that the crank must have a clearance of at least ⅛″ from the top surface. Thus the cranking shaft, including the threaded portion, should protrude at least ¼″ from the top surface. In order to turn the area for housing the movement and also have a closed box, a ¼″-thick portion of the top surface must be cut off. It is, of course, eventually glued back on the box. After the ¼″ top portion is cut off, then the movement hole is turned. The movement hole

should be 1″ deep and have a diameter of at least 2¼″. The diameter is sufficiently large to accommodate the movement base previously measured. The balance of the block is sounding board to which the musical movement will eventually be attached.

4. Before cutting off the ¼″ top portion of the box, sand the surface, then, using a band saw, cut off the top section. In order to align the cut edges later when reassembling, make a pencil mark from top to bottom on one of the sides. If realigned as cut, you will have an almost invisible glue line on all sides of the box.

5. On the base of the box, find the exact center and drill a ⅛″ hole through the box, which hole is for mounting and turning on the short chuck. On the top surface, using the drilled hole as the center point, make a dark circle of 2¼″ diameter. This is the area to be turned.

6. Mount the block on the lathe and turn the movement area to the depth required. In our example this depth is 1″ (Illus. 8-3). Remember to leave a pillar around the lag screw and also to use the tailstock for support. You would be wise to wear a glove when turning this block; if nothing else, be extremely careful when turning, and turn the block at normal lathe speed.

7. After turning, remove the block from the chuck and chisel out the wood pillar. Be certain the base area is flat for proper placement of the movement.

8. Place the crank movement in the exact center of the turned hole and attach it from the inside with small wood screws. The screws should be sufficiently long to hold the movement in place but not penetrate through the base.

9. The next step is marking on the bottom face of the ¼″ cover piece exactly where the crank shaft should penetrate it. Using the pencil alignment marks on the side, carefully line up the fit of the top on the box and press the lid piece onto the crank shaft (Illus. 8-4). The top of the shaft should leave a light mark on the bottom surface of the lid piece. Darken the mark with a pencil so it can be readily found for drilling a hole.

Illus. 8-3 Block Mounted with Movement Area Turned

10. Drill a ⅜″ hole through the mark on the top portion: this is the hole that the cranking shaft will penetrate. Use a sharp wood bit so you do not splinter the top surface around the hole. After drilling, place the top section on the box and check for clearance around the hole and the crank shaft. If the shaft touches the side of the hole when the box edges are aligned, widen the hole until clearance is achieved. Finish-sand the top surface.

11. Blow all dust and particles off the movement and edges of the box and lid. Place yellow glue on

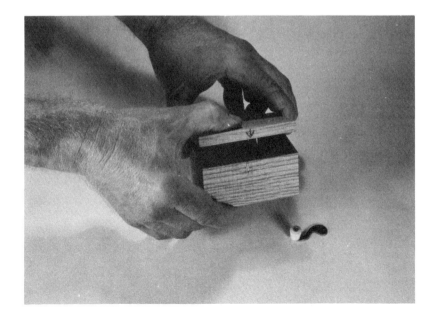

Illus. 8-4 Aligning Top Section of Box on Shaft

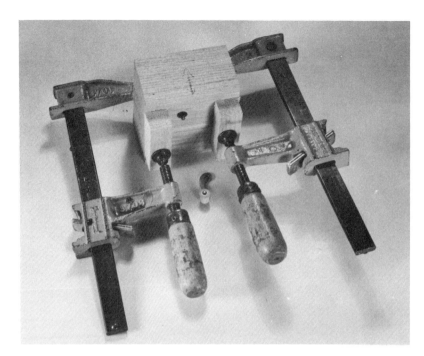

the edges, set the top piece in place and align it carefully, and clamp the assembly until dry (Illus. 8-5).

12. Using a belt sander, if available, finish sanding the box. Roll the edges on both the top and the bottom for a more finished look. Using an air compressor, if available, blow out the dust from the inside of the unit by forcing air through the base chuck hole. Finish the unit as desired, secure the crank, and apply the tune sheet on the base. To allow the clockwork sound to escape, do not cover the chuck hole with the tune sheet.

Design 8-2: The Pine Cranking Music Box (Illus. 8-6)

1. This design uses a standard 2-by-4 pine stud for the top portion of the assembly. The base area is made from standard 1-by-4 pine stock. As you may recall, the actual thickness of a 2-by-4 is 1½″; the thickness of a 1-by-4 board is ¾″.

Cut a round block from the 2-by-4 stock that has a diameter of 3″. From the 1-by-4 material cut another circle with a 3″ diameter. The thinner block will be the eventual base of the unit.

2. The larger block should be attached to a glue block for turning. The smaller block should have a ⅛″ hole drilled through its exact center. The smaller block will be turned on the short chuck, thus the lag screw hole (Illus. 8-7).

3. The small base block must be turned first. After mounting the block on the chuck, bring the tailstock forward to prevent block slippage. It may be necessary to place a shim either in front of or behind the block, depending on the length of the lag screw. Turn the block to shape, removing a minimum of wood. Using a ½″ square nose chisel, cut a shoulder on the top edge, approximately ⅛″ wide and ⅛″ deep, measuring from the top surface. This shoulder is where the top portion of the box will fit and eventually will be glued (Illus. 8-8).

4. Prior to the next turning task, check the dimensions of the movement in relation to the nec-

174

Illus. 8-6 Finished Pine Cranking Box

Illus. 8-7 Pine Blocks Ready for Turning

Illus. 8-8 Turning Pine Base

essary turning tasks. Remember, the cranking shaft must extend from the top of the assembly by at least ¼". The base area that will hold the movement must have a diameter of at least 2¼".

5. In this design, the movement is placed directly on the top surface of the base piece. No area needs to be turned to accommodate it. After removing it from the chuck, you will note that the remaining diameter is more than sufficient to hold the movement.

6. With a faceplate attached to the glue block, shape the outside of the heavier block to the exact diameter of the outer edge of the base unit; use a vernier caliper for this task. Be sure to measure from the wide section of the base and not the cut shoulder area. You may want to round the edge that is attached to the glue block. This eventually will be the top of the box. Next, turn the inside area of the block with a wall that is ⅛" thick, the same as on the base shoulder. The top, attached to the glue block, should also be ⅛" thick (Illus. 8-9).

7. Using abrasive paper, finish the side wall while still on the lathe. Pine is very soft, so be careful not to reduce the outer diameter significantly. Clean up and square the bottom edge.

8. With a parting tool, separate the glue block and the turned piece while on the lathe. Cut primarily into the glue block but also cut the top surface enough to remove the glue and paper mess. If you wish, cut all the way through and grab the piece just as it separates from the glue block. The other option is to leave a ¼" shaft between the glue block and the turned piece and then saw them apart (Illus. 8-10).

9. Remount the base on the chuck and place the top piece on the shoulder. With a small round block between it and the top surface, bring the tailstock forward (Illus. 8-11). This will hold the entire assembly in place and will not damage the top surface. Start the lathe and, with abrasive paper, sand the base and top wall flush, if needed.

10. Using masking tape, tightly wrap tape around the seam between the base and the top. Use enough tape to hold the two together while

Illus. 8-9 Turning Top Section of Pine Box

sanding and, if necessary, lightly cleaning the top surface with a turning tool (Illus. 8-12). Roll the top edge.

11. Place and secure the crank movement in the center of the base area with small wood screws. Carefully set the lid over the movement so its wall aligns with the base shoulder. Press down on the top section so that the crank shaft makes a mark on the inner surface of the top. Mark the indentation with a pencil and then drill a ⅜" hole through the top surface. Test for clearance of the crank shaft from the side of the hole; if necessary, widen the hole for ample clearance.

12. Blow off the sawdust and other particles from the movement, the base, and from the inside of the top section. Place a few drops of white glue on the base shoulder and set the top piece in place, aligning the crank shaft and the hole. Allow the assembly to dry; then finish. I use Watco oil on the pine and then finish the surface with Deft. Attach the crank and the tune sheet.

Illus. 8-10 Parting Glue Block and Turned Top Section

Illus. 8-11 Sanding Base and Top Section Flush

Illus. 8-12 Finishing Top of Box

Design 8-3: The Dome Cranking Music Box (Illus. 8-13)

As noted in Illus. 8-13, this design comprises a base, a dome, and a small knob. The unit is best turned from one of the hardwoods. You may want to do some special preparations with the blocks prior to turning.

1. Prepare a base block that is approximately 1″ (4/4's) thick and has a 3″ diameter. For best results the dome should be roughly 2¼″ (9/4's) thick and also have a 3″ diameter. The knob can be cut from the 1″ (4/4's) stock and have a 1″ diameter.

2. Attach the dome block to a glue block for faceplate turning. The base should have a ⅛″ hole drilled through its exact center for placement on the short chuck. On the top surface of the base, using the hole as a center point, trace a circle with a 2¼″ diameter. The knob block should have a ⅛″

hole drilled in it, approximately ½″ deep (Illus. 8-14).

3. The turning procedures, with a few exceptions, are the same as for the pine design. The dimensions are also the same as for that unit. After turning the shoulder area on the base, this design needs a turned area in that base for holding the movement. Using the 2¼″-diameter circle as a guide, turn an area that is ½″ deep. After turning this area in the base, you should have a ridge between the movement area and the outer shoulder. In this design the entire movement, including the crank, is covered by the dome. The ½″-deep area in the base makes this dimensionally possible.

4. Turn the dome area employing the same pro-

Illus. 8-13 Finished Dome Cranking Music Box

Illus. 8-14 Dome Box Blocks Ready for Turning

cedures as discussed for the pine design. Finish sanding using the tailstock and the tape techniques outlined for Design 8-2.

5. Using a short chuck or screw-center, place a shim between it and the knob block. Turn the knob as desired and finish with abrasive paper.

Using yellow glue, place the knob on the dome and hold in place with a strong rubber band until dry. Finish the assembly, attach the movement with wood screws, place the tune sheet on the base, and begin cranking clockwork music.

Acquiring Music Movements

Woodworkers will find that music movements are readily available from mail order suppliers of woodcrafting materials. Also, suppliers of music movements frequently advertise in woodworking periodicals. A further source of information is The Musical Box Society, International, a nonprofit, international organization dedicated to the enjoyment, study, and preservation of automatic musical instruments. In addition to regularly published materials, the Society offers its membership unique opportunities to learn more about automatic instruments. Annual membership fees are nominal. Individuals desiring more information about the society should write to The Musical Box Society, International, Box 205, Route 3, Morgantown, IN 46160.

INDEX

Metric Equivalents

MM—MILLIMETRES   CM—CENTIMETRES

INCHES TO MILLIMETRES AND CENTIMETRES

INCHES	MM	CM	INCHES	CM	INCHES	CM
1/8	3	0.3	9	22.9	30	76.2
1/4	6	0.6	10	25.4	31	78.7
3/8	10	1.0	11	27.9	32	81.3
1/2	13	1.3	12	30.5	33	83.8
5/8	16	1.6	13	33.0	34	86.4
3/4	19	1.9	14	35.6	35	88.9
7/8	22	2.2	15	38.1	36	91.4
1	25	2.5	16	40.6	37	94.0
1 1/4	32	3.2	17	43.2	38	96.5
1 1/2	38	3.8	18	45.7	39	99.1
1 3/4	44	4.4	19	48.3	40	101.6
2	51	5.1	20	50.8	41	104.1
2 1/2	64	6.4	21	53.3	42	106.7
3	76	7.6	22	55.9	43	109.2
3 1/2	89	8.9	23	58.4	44	111.8
4	102	10.2	24	61.0	45	114.3
4 1/2	114	11.4	25	63.5	46	116.8
5	127	12.7	26	66.0	47	119.4
6	152	15.2	27	68.6	48	121.9
7	178	17.8	28	71.1	49	124.5
8	203	20.3	29	73.7	50	127.0